IF ONLY I COULD *Shut* MY MOUTH

Kimberly Racquel

This book is a work of fiction. All characters appearing in this work are fictitious. Any resemblance to actual events or locales or persons living or dead, is purely coincidental. Names, characters, places and incidents either are products of the author's imagination or are used fictitiously.

Published by PrettyGirlsRead, LLC
Cover Art © 2018 by PrettyGirlsRead, all rights reserved
Cover Layout & Design: HotBookCovers.com

ISBN: 978-0-9887010-2-1

First Printing May 2018
Printed in the United States of America
PrettyGirlsRead™
Atlanta, GA

While writing this book, my husband and sons
jokingly referred to it as the
"Learn to Shut Your Mouth" book.
It tickles me when I think of the title they came up with
since I know there are days when they
want to tell me just that.
I dedicate this to ***my guys****.*
Thanks for your support, patience, and unwavering love.

TABLE OF CONTENTS

PREFACE

I've always had to defend myself. Naively, I thought I was defending myself because of my physical appearance. I guess I'd be considered pretty, or so I've been told, which can cause jealousy and anger from others. You know, pretty hurts. For the longest time, I thought that was the cause and just chalked it up to my looks. However, I've come to the realization that it goes deeper than aesthetics. See, I now understand that I have ***grace*** on my life and simply put, that makes people uncomfortable.

What is this ***grace***, you ask? That's a good question and for years, I was oblivious to its meaning. However, once I started searching for answers, the meaning appeared like an effervescent lightbulb being turned on in a dark room. ***Grace*** is God's special covering. It's UNMERITED FAVOR! That's it. It's simply God's goodness, love, and forgiveness, which like most people, I don't deserve.

There are countless times when God's ***grace*** amazes me. It's hard to believe that he still loves me after I've spit words with enough venom to penetrate a person's heart like a speeding bullet or when I've said horrific things that I wish to take back after mere seconds of the words leaving my mouth. If that isn't his ***grace***, then I don't know what is.

This ***grace***, the type I've been lucky enough to possess, has caused envy, criticism, hatred, eye rolls from women, unwanted advances from horny men, and resentment from those who should have been loving me while protecting me from the dangers of the world. Instead, all I got was pain. So much pain. As a result, I had to protect myself. My weapon of choice? Since my petite frame is barely five-foot-two, I had to find the strongest weapon I could. And, well, my weapon of choice was my mouth, of course. Believe me, it was powerful enough to bring a giant to its knees.

As young as five years old, I could speak my mind which was full of knowledge, thoughts, and opinions, to even the smartest adult. Who would've known I'd need this gift to survive the most traumatic experience of my life? Defenseless, helpless, and alone, my mouth was all I had.

I'd used my mouth to protect myself in so many ways; never knowing when to turn it off. I'd become confrontational, angry, and easily offended with an *'I'm going to get you before you get me'* type attitude. My mouth, and the inability to shut it, has prevented me from enjoying great friendships, destroyed a marriage, caused strife with family, and robbed me of joy and peace. Clearly, my uncontrollable tongue has, at times, done more bad than good.

For years, I thought speaking my mind meant I was strong. Yet, experience has taught me that true strength is being wise enough to keep my mouth closed.

As you read this, I want you to be reminded that I'm far from perfect. This book wasn't written to glorify my growth from a loud mouth attacker to a peace-loving Christian. No, that's not it at all. Instead, I wrote it to help others face their fears and reflect on their childhood with hopes of discovering the events that make them who they are today. This book is for people who want to learn to shut their mouths and let God handle it!

Shutting your mouth is not going to be instinctive, at least not at first. When you first start praying, you won't automatically hear God speaking to you because you're too busy talking. This is going to come from studying the word, having scripture that you can quickly reference in your mind, and then applying it to everyday life. Look at it like this, first you must know the word to live it. I often think of it like a sport and as such, you should practice before you play. It works the same way when shutting your mouth. You must constantly practice your craft and be ready to perform at any given time. Keep an open mind and know that you can learn something from everyone with whom you come in contact, whether you're learning what to say or what NOT to say. **Study. Absorb. Apply. Repeat.** Clearly, it's not easy. If it were, then everyone else would be doing it. Though, if you really want to enjoy ***grace***, live an abundant life, and receive all the blessings God has for you, you will have to do all those things.

As we embark on this journey, you're going to see two sides of my story. First, a flashback to events that shaped my character. Then, the wisdom which resulted from my journal reflections and closer relationship with God.

Remember, there's always a lesson before the blessing.

CHAPTER 1

Everything that makes us who we are stems from childhood. It's where our character and many of our life perceptions begin…

1987 – The Beginning

As young children, we're taught to either speak up or shut up. I've learned that lesson the hard way. It was a muggy August morning and the weatherman forecasted it to be a hundred degrees - typical for weather in Decatur, Georgia during that time of the year. I was ten and it was the first day of school. My age was finally in the double digits and I had to make sure I didn't still look like some measly nine-year-old. Therefore, my hair was no longer curly and bushy, but manageable, bouncy, long, and black thanks to a new Revlon perm that had me feeling sassy.

Envisioning my back to school outfit filled me with so much excitement that I woke up extra early, even before my Mama's alarm clock went off. My red stretch pants, the ones with the stir-ups that went under the feet, perfectly matched the red and black shirt, with a silver star on the front, along with the black bootie shoes my mom bought me from Pic'n Pay. The whole outfit was laid out the night before. Without a doubt, I was going to be 'bustin' or in today's words – sharp and dressed to impress– for my first day of fifth grade at McCoy Elementary School.

Once I got dressed, I couldn't stay out of the mirror as I constantly snapped my neck just so I could feel my newly permed hair bounce. Fitted and ready to go, I picked up my blue JanSport backpack and headed to my parents' room to kiss Daddy and tell him goodbye. As usual, he was still in bed. I headed to the kitchen and grabbed an oddly shaped lumpy biscuit off the stove. Mama wasn't the best cook, but since she tried, I ate it anyway. Anxiously, I sat in my mom's black 1979 Chevrolet Citation and hoped I wouldn't be late for the first day of school. My sister, Andrea, had already been dropped off at Mayfield High School. At seventeen, she was a senior and thought she was grown. Kyle, my baby brother, was also starting his first day of kindergarten and Mama was hurrying to get him ready as well. He was running around, smiling and jumping off of one piece of furniture to the other. I was pretty sure his incessant play was one of the reasons my Mama was taking so long. Finally, after what felt like an eternity, she came out the house and got in the car.

We arrived at school and she walked us in. We went to my class first. She kissed me then grabbed Kyle's hand and headed toward the kindergarten hall. Nervously, I entered the classroom, wondering who was in my class and if my teacher was nice. I glanced around the room and my stomach dropped when I saw Shane, the cute little mixed boy I'd been crushing on since the third grade.

Maury, a disgusting boy with a thick tongue who also sucked his thumb, broke my trance when he jumped up and yelled, "Kira, you can sit by me. Your desk is right here."

Annoyed, I slowly sat at my desk and tried to think of an excuse to get my new teacher to move me somewhere else. Anywhere far away from thick-tongued Maury would be an improvement. Unfortunately for me, my seat assignment would be the least of my worries. As luck would have it, that was the only day I would have to sit next to disgusting Maury.

School let out at two-thirty. I walked over to the kindergarten hall to pick up my brother. Mama was waiting outside. She had a strange look on her face that I'd never forget. Although I'd seen Mama look worried many times, this time was different. Upon entering the car, I could feel something was off.

"Mama, what's wrong?"

She looked at me, tears nearly filling her eyes. "Kira, Andrea done did something terrible up there at that school She's telling a lot of lies on me and Daddy."

Mama

Confusion about your roles as wife and mother left our household out of balance and in shambles. Emotional distress, anguish, and despair cloud your judgment, and everyone connected to you pays the price.

Okay, so I need to go back and give you a little background on my mom. Though slight in stature, she was a curvaceous five-two and about a hundred-twenty pounds of all woman. Her smooth skin was the color of those little square caramel candies that you could only find around Christmas. Soft, sandy brown shoulder length hair framed her pecan brown eyes. Not being the girly type, she never wore perfume. Yet, she had a signature fragrance of Keri lotion mixed with cigarette smoke. Old photographs tell the story of her high school popularity as a track star. She even made history in her school for being the youngest girl to ever make Varsity cheerleader. Mama was my first idol. However, beauty, popularity, and track medals could never compensate for her struggles with low self-esteem.

Mama was the product of a loveless marriage between two people whose misery infected everyone around them, including their only daughter. As a young girl, she painfully watched my grandfather be emasculated by my Grandma Helen who berated and belittled him for sport. With nowhere to run, my grandfather sought a haven in alcohol, drinking himself into drunken stupors on a regular basis. Trapped inside their turmoil, Mama was emotionally abandoned and unloved. This left a void in her life that she filled with insecurity which left her yearning for love and acceptance; things she thought she could find in a man. Blind to her own self-worth, she couldn't recognize the signs of a man who wasn't prepared to be a husband or a father.

Coming from a lonely childhood, Mama wasn't happy unless she was in a relationship – no matter how unhealthy. She believed love could conquer all and foolishly accepted my father's unreliable income and inconsistent leadership as head of our household. Coupled with all these shortcomings, struggling was inevitable. Many times, the only food in the refrigerator was lettuce and mayonnaise. I'd sprinkle black pepper on top to give it a better taste. It rarely worked but it was worth a shot.

When the gas bill didn't get paid, we'd boil water on the stove and use it to wash ourselves. Quickly, we'd hit all the pertinent body parts while the water was warm and anything else just got a quick once over with a cold washrag. Kyle would go first since he was the youngest and smallest. Then, I'd get in and share his water. By the time I finished, the next pot would be heated so that Andrea and mom could share the water. Daddy always got his own round of pots even though he was the one responsible for the gas getting cut off in the first place.

It wasn't all bad though. The happiest I'd ever seen Mama was when Daddy moved us to a nice three-bedroom house in Decatur. She converted the third bedroom into our family den. Man, I loved that den! Gathering in front of the television and playing Atari or watching movies together on Friday nights made me feel as if we were the Huxtables – perfect and content. On family nights, I'd closely watch Mama to see if she was happy. As always, she seemed to only be concerned about Daddy and if he was having a good time. If he was happy, then she was happy.

Our living room was the one place in the house where her smile wasn't dependent on my father's mood. Mama had saved up every last penny on a white velvet sofa with red feathery throw pillows. And for that reason, us kids with our snotty noses and dirty fingerprints, weren't allowed to step foot in that room. She never said it, but the furniture was her trophy – something that made her immensely proud.

Outside was Mama's favorite place. We had a huge backyard with a swing set. Kyle loved the slide, while I preferred to sit in the grass and write in my journal instead of helping Mama and Andrea hang clothes on the clothesline. Writing allowed me to escape into my own world even if my feet never left the comforts of our backyard.

Appearance was everything so Mama did her best to keep us in style and looking nice. The kitchen was our makeshift salon where she washed our hair at the sink before giving us a stove-side press. That is, until she finally gave in to the creamy crack craze and allowed me to get a perm for the first day of fifth grade.

Christmas was Mama's favorite holiday and she made sure we got everything on our list even if it meant taking a second job at Lionel Playworld, the neighborhood toy store. She had dreams of becoming a nurse and eventually enrolled in college. Sadly, she ended up dropping out because working a full-time job, taking classes in the evening, raising us, and supporting Daddy, were too much for her to do on her own. Overall, Mama did the very best she could and tried to make the most with what she had.

Proverbs 14:1 "A wise woman builds her house, but a foolish woman tears it down with her own hands."

As a little girl, Mama was my idol. However, once I got older and had children of my own, journaling revealed my determination to be a different type of mother. Mixed up priorities impaired her ability to understand the delicate balance of being a wife, running a household, and keeping close watch over her children. A mother's primary role is to nurture her offspring with love, support, and understanding. Instead, Mama chose to raise her grown husband. Thus, her infatuation with being a wife, made her fail as a mother which should have been her most important role.

Growing up, my identity was lost. It was as if I was walking down a long dark hall opening door after door in search of my purpose. Hoping for somewhere to belong. Probing for safety. There wasn't anyone to build me up and point out my talents or guide me in the direction of my purpose. I wouldn't wish that sort of pain on my worst enemy and I certainly didn't want to bestow it upon my children. So, my early life gives me the determination to not only be there for my sons but to be a presence in their lives. Because I lacked love as a child, I know how it stings when your name is announced in an auditorium of proud parents yet no one is there to applaud for you. I promised my sons would never experience that empty hollow. So, when I attend their plays, performances, or award ceremonies, and I see them smile brightly as they search for my face in a crowd of mothers, I'm reminded that everything I'd gone through was not in vain. Inevitably, it helped me create the life they so deserved.

Being raised without a mother's love left a void in my life and was one of the hardest things I've ever endured. While in the midst of it, I never understood why I had to deal with such turmoil. However, the love with which I now shower my sons, fills that void for me. I no longer view my childhood trauma as a curse. In fact, it was a blessing in disguise. Because of it, I was bestowed with insight into the importance of nurturing. It gives me the strength and wisdom needed to raise boys to become men. I've been given a special assignment, to nurture young kings who would one day create life and be the heads of their own households. Now, I realize it was meant to help mold and shape my sons. Hindsight is always 20/20, I guess.

Tuesdays are exclusively reserved for my children. During this time, my prayers and journaling are solely focused on them. Speaking affirmations for their present and their future is an essential component of my routine. Writing about their special qualities enables me to recognize their unique talents and identify purposeful ways to encourage, nourish, and help them flourish. Journaling provides an acceptance that my role as a parent will undergo many stages and transitions. During their early years, I wanted them to grow up so quickly. Diapers and daycare were tiresome and as a young mother, I felt boggled down. Now, through journaling and quiet reflection, I can see that God wants me to take pleasure in my maternal duty. See it as a blessing instead of a burden. As my sons get older, I'm beginning to enjoy our conversations and their ability to challenge me intellectually. I'm their spiritual leader and by shutting my mouth instead of complaining, I'm able to make sure my spirit is intact.

CHAPTER 2

At first, I thought Andrea told the school about our parents fighting all the time. See, Daddy and Mama had lots of arguments about money. I figured out quickly that my dad's unsteady employment made it very hard on us. I thought my sister may have run her mouth about us not having food in the house or how my Daddy stole one thing after another.

Daddy never had money or a job for that matter. But, I remember him hustling up a few dollars once. He came home and promised me I could get anything I wanted. I had been eyeing a burgundy Members Only jacket and begged him to get it. Later that night, my Daddy came home and said he had a surprise for me. This was very odd because we only got presents for Christmas and were lucky to get anything for our birthdays. He called me into his bedroom and passed me a wrapped box. I tore that sucker open like the Tasmanian Devil, just shredding paper everywhere. Then, my eyes nearly popped out of the socket. It was the burgundy Members Only jacket. I leapt to my feet and screamed with excitement. I couldn't wait to wear it for the first day of school along with my Jordache jeans and Etonics tennis shoes. Finally, my Daddy came through for me. Usually, the most he had ever given me were his old church socks to use as makeshift clothes for my Barbie dolls. But this time, he actually bought me something. It was a moment of pride.

I went to bed that night, like usual, but when I woke up the next morning and opened my closet to admire my now favorite jacket, it was gone. I shifted the rack of clothes from left to right but still, no jacket. I checked the floor, my hamper, under the bed – but still, no jacket.

Defeated and hysterical, I burst into my parents' room. "Mama, have you seen my Members Only jacket?"

"Don't tell me you lost that jacket, Kira," my mother snapped.

"No, of course not, it was hanging in my closet. I put it there before I went to sleep."

Hesitantly, she got up and walked over to my room. She scoured the clothes but couldn't find my jacket either. Then something struck me like a bolt of lightning running through my veins. I ran back to my parents' room and shook my Daddy awake.

When he opened his eyes, I yelled, "Daddy, where is my jacket?"

His dropped chin and lowered eyes said what his words couldn't admit. He knew.

Again, I pleaded, "Daddy, where is my jacket?"

"Kira," he averted my gaze as he spoke. "Daddy had to borrow your jacket for a little change to pay a bill. I'll have it back to you by the end of the week."

Devastation. Hurt. Pain. Disappointment. Feelings no child should endure, overcame every nerve in my body. That was the first of many times when Daddy made me realize that the only man I could depend on was God because all others were bound to disappoint.

I never saw that jacket again. The days that followed were full of sadness – not from me but from Daddy. His depression kept him from holding a steady job and we often went without the bare necessities. This really bothered me but what irked me even more was the fact that my mom kept allowing it. Things got worse and the arguments grew more intense. Eventually, everything my parents bought either got pawned or taken back to the store to get the cash. Goodbye, Atari. So long, colored television. I never got attached to anything because chances were high that I wouldn't have it for long.

After a while, Mama got tired of us going without food and hot water so she began lying to Daddy about having money. Since she wasn't forking over her earnings anymore, he'd go behind her back and forge her name on checks before she realized the money was missing. This caused even more financial problems, with bad checks bouncing higher than a quarter being dropped on a tight bed sheet. To save what little credit she had, Mama started hiding her checkbook. Being a money grubbing super sleuth, Daddy always found it which made changing her hiding spots, at least twice a day, a regular occurrence. Lucky for Mama, I had a photographic memory so I remembered every new spot even when she had forgotten.

Being my little observant self, I spotted Daddy spying on Mama as she changed her hiding spot one day. His eyes lit up as he thought about getting his hands on that checkbook. Clearly, he had big plans. Knowing if he got his greasy paws on her checks that we'd end up boiling bath water again, I had to do everything in my power to make sure he didn't. As soon as he went to the bathroom, I darted out my room and hid the checkbook in the bottom of my toy box. There was no way he'd look there.

When Mama left for work the next morning, his rambling began. Daddy was never up that early, especially on a Saturday, but he had plans to find that checkbook. Having no luck with his search, he knocked on my door.

Daddy fidgeted from side to side as he asked, "Kira, do you know where Mama put her checks?"

"No Daddy, I don't."

"Kira, I know you know. You watch everything that goes on around here." He pleaded for a clue while scratching his neck like bugs were crawling on him. "I really need that checkbook."

I loved my Daddy but I loved hot bath water a little more, so I kept my mouth shut. I think he knew I wasn't going to budge because eventually he stopped trying.

"I understand, you're right to protect your Mama. You're a good girl."

He closed the door to my room and gave up on his hunt. Andrea watched on in disgust but never said a word. Surely she told her school about my Daddy trying to take Mama's money or so I thought. Little did I know, what she said was much worse than that.

Daddy

Running from manhood and responsibility, you married for stability and a soft landing place. Your spiritual walk into manhood in its infancy. No leadership, provision, or protection. You left me fatherless.

Well, I guess you need a little background on Daddy now. Other than being about two shades lighter than a brown paper sack, Daddy was a dead ringer for Philip Michael Thomas. Yes, the guy who played Ricardo Tubbs, on the 80's television show, *Miami Vice*. A well-groomed mustache, beard, and goatee was all he needed to command the attention of every woman he passed by. Thankfully, I inherited his good looks. When people would see him and then see me, they'd say he couldn't deny me even if he wanted. I was his doppelganger.

He covered his wavy jet-black hair with baseball caps that snap in the back, the kind that hung on gas station registers. Brut cologne was his signature scent. I thought he was so handsome, and despite his flaws, I was proud that he was my Daddy. While he shaved and brushed his beard I'd sit on the floor, in the hallway outside of the bathroom, and talk to him. He listened to every word as though everything I said, even my childish gibberish, was important. Every time he walked through the door, he'd serenade me with the lyrics to One Way's song. *"Cutie Pie, you're the reason why…"*. To this day, whenever I hear that song, a euphoric nostalgia fills my heart.

Daddy was a family-loving country boy turned city slicker. Unlike Mama, he was raised in a tight-knit, loving and supportive family. My grandfather was a mild-mannered church going man who wore the pants in his household. My dad was the seventh of eight children, yet he was treated like the baby of the siblings. My grandmother was a very traditional woman who stayed home and raised her family.

We went to visit my grandparents every Christmas and would stay overnight. After my grandfather died, I'd sleep with my Big Mama, the name we called my dad's mom, so that we could wake up early to make biscuits. At the crack of dawn, I'd get up and roll the dough with a drinking glass while listening to stories about my dad when he was a young boy. I distinctly remember, in every story, Big Mama always said Daddy was the only child she had to worry about. He was the one who required ongoing encouragement to complete the smallest tasks. She always wondered if he would ever be a man who could stand on his own two feet. Even at my young age, I wondered the same.

My parents met when Mama went to pick up her friend, Tricia, who just happened to be my dad's cousin. As the story goes, Mama pulled up to the house and honked the horn. Tricia came outside to get in the car, but before they could drive away, my dad emerged and asked if he could get a ride to the west side of town. Because he had the nerve to ask for a ride instead of a date, Mama should have left him right there. But, I guess I wouldn't be here had she done that.

Don't get the wrong idea and roll a disdainful eye toward my Daddy. He'd give you his last, as long as he didn't have to work for it. Honestly, he'd even hand you the shirt off his back. Even though he didn't hold down a steady job, he made sure we were well taken care of while Mama worked long hours. Cooking dinner, helping with homework, and making sure our things were ready for school the next day were the many ways he pulled his weight around the house. Daddy even combed my hair from time to time and I'd sweet talk him into letting me wear it loose on the ends. When one of us kids got sick, he wouldn't leave our side. He was loving to me, my brother, and my sister, Andrea – despite her not being his biological daughter. He loved us all and although it wasn't enough to fill the void caused by my mother's detachment, it helped me feel somewhat special.

1 Timothy 5:8 "But if anyone does not provide for his own, and especially for those of his household, he has denied the faith and is worse than an unbeliever..."

Daddy didn't understand that as a man, it was his responsibility to lead, protect, and provide. The last thing I was going to do was marry a man like my father. Luckily, now that I'm a grown woman, I've been blessed to find someone who understands what it means to be a man. He knows how to provide and fully accepts the role that God designed for him. My husband is everything that a man should be. Unfortunately, I didn't get it right the first time around as I'm currently on my second marriage. Eventually, I'll explain how I got here. But for now, let me gloat about this man that God sent to save me from myself.

Men are inherently designed to be the foundations of their home. Breadwinners. Spiritual leaders. Protectors. Role models. My husband, Mark, is not only passionate about serving others and his community but he's also a wonderful example to my sons. He models manhood, responsibility, hard work, as well as love for his family and God without an ounce of shame. Every attribute that I once feared my sons wouldn't acquire from their biological father, Mark possesses. All the qualities that were never present in my Daddy are fabrics woven into Mark's character.

While journaling, I'd write down all the attributes I wanted in a man. I'd scribe of my father's ineptitude and the disappointment I felt every time he fell short of his paternal obligations. Prayer led me to Mark. In the solace of my thoughts, devoid of the labors of my tongue, I manifested the perfect man and then God brought him to life. My parents taught me how dysfunctional a relationship can be when the roles are reversed and the man follows the woman's lead. However, with Mark, I've learned how to equally embark on a path that brings us – as husband and wife – closer together.

CHAPTER 3

We arrived home and Mama told us to go sit down in the den and watch cartoons while she made some phone calls. Speculating caused my stomach to ache with fear. From the den, I eavesdropped on Mama's conversation. My little brother kept running his mouth so I covered it with my hand and continued listening. I didn't miss a word.

The first call she made was to my sister's school. The counselor claimed that Andrea accused my father of abusing her. My ear hustling had left me in disbelief. Could Andrea have actually done something like this? What does all this mean exactly?

A couple of days prior, she hinted that she had *'something for Daniel'*. That was the way she put it. Her lips curled into a devilish sneer while telling me she'd get him back for being so strict and not letting her go to the school dance with her boyfriend, Tyrone. But, my parents thought he was trouble since he already had two young babies. The one time they let her go out on a date with him, he brought her back way past curfew and my parents were worried sick. Maybe, I should've opened my mouth and warned my mother about her remarks. However, I didn't take her seriously supposing she was just making idle threats.

After my mother hung up the phone, she called Tricia and vented about the whole situation. Pacing back and forth while chain-smoking her nicotine sticks, she repeated the same words over and over again. "I cannot believe Andrea did this."

As soon as she hung up the phone with Tricia, it rang again. I then heard a faint hint of surrender in my mother's voice as she hesitantly said, "Ok, I'll be down there."

Mom came into the den and told me and Kyle to put on our shoes. She said Andrea was in Decatur at the DFACS office. My heart leapt with the kind of fear you feel when you are unexpectedly dropped ten stories in a parachute. What in the world is DFACS? I didn't quite know what they did at the Department of Family and Children's Services but I knew it wasn't a good place for my sister to be. I also knew I didn't want to go. Everything inside of me screamed, **NO! DON'T GO DOWN THERE. STAY HOME.**

I begged my mother to drop us off at Tricia's house like she often did when she needed a babysitter.

"Just pick us up tonight when you get done," I pleaded.

"No." She was firm. "They want me to bring you down so they can ask you some questions."

My stomach dropped yet again but this time like I was falling fifty stories down to a cement ground. To say I was freaking out, would put it mildly. I wanted to run and hide. What would they want to ask me? Questions racked my brain. What has my sister told them about me? Why did she do this? Was she serious about her devious threat just days earlier?

The ride to DFACS was like going to my own funeral. Out of frustration, Mama hit the steering wheel when she saw the **Paid Parking Only** sign. Since we barely had money for the gas it took to get there and surely didn't have enough to pay for the parking lot, we parked a block away before trekking to the office. Holding Mama's trembling hand and sensing her fear, I pleaded with her not to make me go. I had an awful feeling that I wouldn't see her again but she kept gently pulling me along.

"Kira, these people will come and get you if I don't bring you down here," she explained.

We rode the elevator up to the fourth floor where we were met by a Caucasian woman who introduced herself as our

Case Worker, Judy Dillan. I wondered what the heck a caseworker was and why on Earth we needed one.

She reached her pale hand out to me, and said, "Hi, Kira, let's go to my office so that I can ask you some questions." Then, she whispered to my mom, "We will only keep her for three days."

Wait! What did I just hear? Three days? Keep me? Why? How many questions could she possibly ask me that would take three days? This is when I felt I had to take action.

"NO!" I snatched my hand away from Ms. Dillan's and ran like Flo Jo, toward the door, right past Mama.

I had to reach Daddy and tell him what was going on. He'd protect me. He wouldn't let them ask me questions and no way in hell would he let them keep me for three days. Before the elevator door opened, I felt a hand on my shoulder. It was Mama. She turned me around and hugged me. I broke down crying. I was holding on to her so tight. I could smell the Kerry lotion and cigarettes. I wanted to stay right there, safely in her arms and inhaling her scent.

She whispered in my ear, "Remember what I always told you, the family that prays together, stays together. God will protect us and God will protect you. Just go with the lady, answer her questions, and you'll be back home in three days."

I had no choice. So, I walked back into the lobby area where Ms. Dillan was waiting with an extended hand. I stepped forward and followed her through a tall door with tears burning my eyes. I looked back at Mama who mouthed, “I love you.” I’ll never forget the look on her face as she said it. The look was pure hopelessness. The door shut hard. **Loud. Fast. Final.** I knew that would be the last time I’d see my Mama.

We walked to the room at the furthest end of the hall. It was empty except for two chairs. Ms. Dillan encouraged me to have a seat. Wanting to exert what little control I had, I refused. Unbothered by my defiant gesture, she shut the door leaving me standing there alone. I paced and cried. After a while, the door opened and in walked Andrea. Her look wasn’t hopeless like Mama’s. Instead, her face was an image of shock, then fret. Bursting into a waterfall of tears, she ran toward me and grabbed me into a bear hug.

“It was supposed to be just me,” she wailed.

I didn’t understand what she meant. All I knew was that something terrible was happening to our family and I wanted my Daddy. Rewinding and replaying my avalanche of thoughts, I demanded an explanation from Andrea.

“Does all of this have something to do with what you told me a couple of weeks ago?”

Beads of sweat pooled at her temple. She couldn’t undo what she’d already done and now she had to answer for it. “Yeah,I told them Daniel has been touching me.”

Andrea

My first best friend. My first enemy. My hero and my villain. Everything you were supposed to be has somehow been tainted. Instead of sharing some of the best memories, we shared some of the worst. Yet, I still cling to our bond. After all, we are sisters.

Growing up, Janet Jackson was my sister's idol. When she wore her black shoulder length hair in a side swept ponytail, she looked just like Janet on the *Control* album cover. Andrea was voluptuous for her age with chestnut cinnamon colored skin and a big round booty that got her lots of attention. My sister was boy crazy and was always sneaking away to meet up with boys every chance she got. She even went as far as tongue kissing the preacher's oldest son in the backroom at Grandma Helen's church.

Pretending to go to school events, she'd sneak off with boys. Punishment only made her work harder to get around my parents' rules. The last straw was when my mom found black lingerie in her book bag. It turns out instead of going to her high school's playoff football game, she had plans to go to a hotel with her boyfriend, Tyrone.

Clearly, there was a deeper issue. As I mentioned before, our character and life perceptions stem from childhood. Andrea was my half-sister, six-and-a-half years older than me, but only sixteen years younger than our mother. Still a kid herself, Mama wasn't ready to be a mother. Andrea only got in the way of her quest to find a man. So, what do many teenage mothers do when they aren't ready to be mothers? They throw all the responsibility onto someone else and keep it moving. My grandmother Helen saw this as her chance to finally get parenthood right so she gladly took on the duties.

Andrea and Mama were more like sisters than mother and daughter. Couple that with virtually no relationship with her biological father, my sister was attention starved. Then by the time I came along, Mama was focused on landing Daddy and thus, Andrea was pushed to the side once again. Seeking attention wherever she could get it, she was willing to break rules to get to the arms of the first guy who showed interest. Punishment was the only way my parents knew to control her so they removed every privilege possible, including her Sweet Sixteen party.

It was always a give and take situation. My parents would take away her freedom and she would give the gift of her absence by running off somewhere. One time, she ran away and after three days, my parents were worried sick. Desperate to be consoled, Mama called Grandma Helen. She was sure her mother would be there for her during this crisis. And she was right. Grandma Helen stepped up. She prayed for Mama and they talked on the phone for hours. Their relationship was finally healing. It's amazing how a crisis has a way of bringing a family together.

However, the supportive grandmother role would be short lived. By day five, my mother was emotionally exhausted. The police, family, and friends were looking everywhere for my sister. Then the phone rang. I couldn't hear what Mama was saying because the door to my room was shut. Suddenly, my mom burst in with a wild look on her face. "Kira, put your shoes on and find something for Kyle to wear. We're going to get Andrea. She has been at your Grandma Helen's house the whole time!"

Exodus 20:16 "You shall not bear false witness…"

Somewhere along the way, Andrea learned that lying gets you what you want. Telling the truth never came to her mind. As her younger sister, I wanted to be just like her, that is, until I got older and became aware that I could never dress myself in the cloak of deception Andrea wore every day. It was too heavy a burden. Rarely at peace, Andrea was always either crafting a lie or covering one. This taught me to tell the truth. It just seemed easier. Freeing even. Yes, sometimes the truth that came from my mouth hurt others, but because it was the truth, that discomfort was only temporary. Lies, on the other hand, have long-lasting effects, some of which are devastating and irreversible.

CHAPTER 4

"Messing with you how?" I asked."Grandma Helen said I should tell my teacher that he hits me on my butt and makes me do things," Andrea admitted without a sense of remorse.

I was dazed and confused. I couldn't understand how her lies placed us in this situation. But, when she mentioned Grandma Helen, I knew things were about to get a whole lot worse.

Grandma Helen

The gatekeeper of generational curses. Committing all the sins of a mother. Your hate, manipulation, and cruelty caused so much pain and destruction. It's unforgivable.

Grandma Helen was a beauty anomaly with her dark milk-chocolate skin, sultry eyes, and long silky black hair. She attracted men by the droves but only had eyes for one and I'm not talking about my grandfather. Her reverse color complex made her despise anyone lighter than her dark brown hue. She cheated on grandpa with a man the color of motor oil who us kids called Big Jimmy.

Grandma Helen stood only four-foot-nine, but had the cruelty of Goliath. Hate was all I ever got from her as she made it a practice to play favorites between me and Andrea. Not only did she detest me, she also loathed my Daddy and made sure we both knew it. Since emasculating men was her specialty, she was determined to tear my father down every chance she got. If she couldn't find something to criticize, she'd roll her eyes and give him a death stare. If she could find a way to kill him and get away with it, she would have and there's no way I'd think otherwise.

Since my mother's main priority was spending alone time with Daddy, she'd frequently ask my grandmother to babysit us. During those visits, Grandma Helen forced me to sit on the sofa while everyone was up and running about. I couldn't even get up to use the restroom. At dinner time, instead of allowing me to sit at the kitchen table with her and Andrea, she'd isolate me like a puppy placing my plate on the floor in the corner of an adjacent room. Making me face the wall was her way of punishing me for being light skinned. She'd then load my plate with mounds of food and dare me to get up before my entire meal was gone. When I didn't eat all my food, she'd force feed me until I gagged. After a while, my defiance would kick in and I'd let the food run down the sides of my mouth. We did this all night until she heard my parents' car turn down her dead-end street. Then, and only then, she'd allow me to get up.

Trepidation made me pretend as though nothing happened. Andrea witnessed all of this and didn't attempt to stop her or help me. Wasn't my big sister supposed to be my hero? Unfortunately for me, as long as Andrea was treated like a princess, she was okay with turning a blind eye to the cruel treatment I endured. Eventually, I told Mama but she made me promise not to tell my Daddy. For one, she didn't want my mistreatment to interfere with her ever important date nights. Secondly, she and Grandma Helen had their own deep-rooted issues. So, this was just another ingredient to be added to their recipe of unspoken problems.

Grandma Helen did some of the sneakiest things to Mama which only made life harder. For instance, Andrea's biological father had dropped child support payments at my grandmother's house for over thirteen years. Instead of handing them over to my mom, my grandmother secretly cashed them and kept the money to herself. It wasn't until Mama opened a child support case that she found Andrea's father had been making payments all the time.

That's just how she was. She was good at keeping secrets and would take the biggest secret ever to her grave. Saying she was jealous of Mama would be an understatement. Because she caused so much drama, Daddy insisted that we move across town to create some distance between our family and the problems she created for us. Moving to Decatur was a big deal back then. An upward status move. No longer would we be living in an apartment on the west side of Atlanta where break-ins and robberies were common place. We were moving up like *The Jeffersons.* Furious about our move, Grandma Helen refused to visit.

Over the first few months in our home, Mama had worked hard, saving money to buy a white velvet living room sofa set and she wanted my grandmother to see it. Finally, she decided to pay us a visit. As she toured our new house, she stayed mute with the exceptional hateful eye rolls for which she had been known. Afterwards, she spent the day with us and seemed to be a little pleasant. As the night went on though, things regressed – big time.

Having finished dinner, we were cleaning up the kitchen. Mama and Andrea were washing dishes and Grandma Helen was scraping leftovers out of the pots and pans. Suddenly, she grabbed a big black cast iron skillet, the one that every African-American family uses to fry chicken. Speaking aloud, to no one in particular, she yelled, "You and that high yellow nigga think y'all better than me, don't you?"

Before we could figure out who she was talking to, she marched into our living room, cast iron skillet in hand. Mama, Andrea, and me followed behind her trying to see what she was about to do. Right before our very eyes, she threw hot chicken grease all over Mama's white living room sofa. My mother was frozen, tears streaming down her face. Andrea stood speechless watching the grease soak into Mama's sofa.

I broke the silence. "I'm gonna tell my Daddy!"

As she turned toward me, she squinted her eyes and said, "Tell him."

She grabbed her purse off the end table, threw on her coat, and walked out the door. It slammed hard behind her. Mama sat on the floor in front of her grease-stained white sofa sobbing. I couldn't wait for Daddy to get back home. It was time for him to know everything my grandmother had been putting us through. Andrea begged me not to tell. I had no idea why she'd still want to protect that hellish woman after all that.

When my father got home, his jaw dropped to the floor. By this time, Grandma Helen was long gone and Mama was still sitting on the floor crying. I told him everything that happened that day including how she treated me when they weren't around. After this incident, Daddy didn't let me go to her house anymore but he didn't stop Andrea. He knew that Grandma Helen had practically raised her before he even came in the picture so he didn't think it was fair to prohibit her visits.

Thus, giving Grandma Helen more one on one time with Andrea and even more influence to make her do all the bad things to my Daddy that she couldn't do herself. Looking back, perhaps Andrea got too close to Grandma Helen.

Though the visits stopped, there were still familial functions where my grandmother appeared. On the rare occasions where we had a barbecue, Daddy was extremely vocal toward Grandma Helen when he'd catch her giving me that evil stare of hers. Normally, he was mild mannered, but when it came to protecting his family, he didn't play. Obviously, Grandma Helen knew he was serious because she opted to pretty much avoid me altogether. Still, she was determined to make sure I knew how she felt about me, and whenever the opportunity presented itself, she'd whisper insults and threats to me through clenched teeth.

Eventually, Mama's desire to have time with her man made her plead with Daddy to let Grandma Helen babysit us again. Because he lacked a backbone, Daddy ultimately gave in. Once back in my grandmother's care, she replaced the force feeding with threats to backhand slap my yellow face. As her hate for me escalated, so did her insults with her calling me every high yella' whore in the book. Nothing was off limits which was evident with her constant degrading of my dad. According to her, he was a no-good nigga who wasn't ever going to be worth a red cent.

The days at Grandma Helen's house were relentless but the babysitting would end abruptly. Unfortunate for Kyle, there would be dire consequences. Two wide cement steps led up to the front door of her house. There was a drop off so steep, we'd practically lunge just to step up. Left alone outside, my brother and I played on the front porch. Grandma Helen and Andrea were in the house, talking in normal tones at first, but then lowering their voices to whispers. My nosy radar went into high alert and my ears piqued to hear every word. I tiptoed to the door and leaned against the screen. Just when I settled my body in a good position to hear everything, there was an agonizing scream. It was Kyle. He'd managed to push his toy car to the edge of the porch and had fallen down the cement steps, scraping the skin on the side of his face from his eyebrow to his chin.

Andrea was the first one to belt out the door followed closely by Grandma Helen. Blood was everywhere. When Andrea picked him up, his screams pierced through the hot Georgia air like a knife. I was afraid that everyone on the entire street would hear him. Andrea lunged upstairs and bolted into the house. From the corner of my eye, I noticed Grandma Helen casually strolling behind us, not panicked one bit. Unconcerned about Kyle, she immediately began to construct a lie for my sister to tell Mama and Daddy. I was shaking and scared because I thought he was going to die by the way he was flinching each time the peroxide-soaked cotton ball touched his now skinless face. Instead of calling an ambulance, they carefully crafted their story.

By the time my parents arrived, my grandmother and Andrea had their stories down pact. Grandma Helen warned she'd kill me if I opened my mouth. With all the evil and hate inside of her I believed her threats, but since my brother's life was at stake, I didn't care. Daddy took one look at Kyle and all hell broke loose. He was fuming, quizzing them like an episode of *Columbo*. His eyebrows raised in disbelief as they spieled one lie after the other. He knew there wasn't an ounce of truth coming out of their mouths. Meanwhile, Grandma Helen and Andrea stood firm with their fib. They said we were all sitting outside and Kyle moved too fast for them to catch him. The words just flowed from their deceitful tongues. No hesitation. No remorse.

As we were leaving, Grandma Helen insisted that Andrea spend the night but Mama, who up until that point said nothing, finally chimed in with a firm no. Before we left, my eyes locked with my grandmother's. Her expression said it all – she was going to kill me if I opened my mouth and told the truth.

Usually, her gaze was enough to scare me into silence but this time, she couldn't pump enough fear into me to make me shut my mouth. After waiting just long enough to get to the expressway, I sang like a caged bird. My sister pinched me hard to make me shut up. I swatted her hand and kept talking.

Mama directed her line of questioning to Andrea. I sensed she knew full well Andrea was lying. Just to make sure though, I refuted everything she said and even explained how they spent hours concocting their story.

Before we made it home, I dropped one more bomb. "Daddy, Grandma Helen told me she was going to kill me for telling."

Daddy almost swerved off the highway. He was fuming.

Mama only shook her head in disbelief and mumbled, "I just can't believe my Mama."

The phone was ringing as soon as we got home. Mama yelled to my sister to answer it. Meanwhile, she quietly picked up the receiver in her bedroom. She overheard Grandma Helen telling Andrea to stick with their story.

Finally, Mama was fed up. Interrupting their conversation my mother screamed, "Why Mama? Why do you keep doing this to me? You have never loved me. I've been fooling myself my whole life and you keep making a fool of me. I'm done. Stay away from me and my family."

Grandma Helen responded loud enough so we all heard her through the phone, "You can keep that little high yellow heifer and that no-good nigga, but Andrea, she's mine. I promise you that!"

Proverbs 15:4 "A gentle tongue is a tree of life, but perverseness in it breaks the spirit..."

Grandma Helen's cruel treatment, judgment, and criticism, ignited my private battle with insecurity. I didn't realize it until I tried to journal about her and found myself staring at an empty page. I just couldn't find any words to express my feelings toward the vilest woman I'd ever encountered. All I knew was that she was the one responsible for breaking my spirit. Because of her, I didn't believe in myself.

CHAPTER 5

As Andrea and I stood in the room, I couldn't help but wonder what would happen next. I had plenty of questions and was ready for Ms. Dillan to come back to give me some answers. Then, the door opened. Before I had a chance to speak, she was already doling out instructions.

"I'm going to take you all to a place where you'll be safe and can sleep for the night."

"Why can't we go home?" I asked.

"Because tomorrow you'll have to come back down here for questioning."

My heart stopped. "Where are you taking us then?"

As if she'd answered the same question a thousand times before, she callously responded, "To an Emergency Shelter."

The shelter was an old elementary school converted into a youth home for children suffering from traumatic family crises. Upon arrival, we were greeted by a lady with toffee colored skin. She introduced herself as Ms. Jackson and proceeded to show us around the shelter. As we were touring the facilities, she held my chin in her hand, lifted my face toward the light, and said, "You're the prettiest little girl I've ever seen. Stop crying. Don't mess up that angelic face."

Her gentle and warm auntie type personality calmed me down a bit. Heading to a small room that contained pre-packed linen, she gave each of us a folded towel and washcloth, a thin, white flannel nightgown with pink flowers on it, a change of underwear, and some hospital issued blue socks with the no-slip bottoms. The only clothes we had were the ones we wore to school. I didn't want to take a shower because I wanted to keep wearing my brand new outfit. Most of all, I just wanted to go back to my own house. I knew Daddy would be worried sick when he came home and realized we weren't there.

"Can we go home?" I asked.

"I'm sorry baby, you can't." Ms. Jackson knelt so that we were seeing eye to eye. "Let me show you where the showers are."

We entered a bathroom that had about six shower stalls lined up in a row. Since we always took baths at home, this new concept of standing to bathe was foreign to me.

"Where is the bathtub, Ms. Jackson?"

"We don't have bathtubs; we only have showers. Get in. I'll be back in 20 minutes."

Was I supposed to just take my clothes off right there in the middle of this open, cold bathroom? Where are the rugs? What do I step out on?

Sensing my hesitation, Andrea grabbed my hand and led me to a shower stall. She pushed back the clear, see-through curtain and turned the water on.

"Come on Kira. It's just like a bath but you gotta stand up instead. You still wash the same way."

I was mortified. It felt like one of those scenes out of a women's prison show. It wasn't that I was afraid of the shower, I just felt that once I got in, I would be one step further away from home. The waves of warm water hitting my body alerted me that I had crossed over into a whole new world. Suddenly, those boiled pot water baths didn't seem so bad. Retrospectively, they symbolized that we were family and we were together no matter what problem we faced. But now, standing in the shower, I was forced to fight my battle alone. No longer protected by the safety of family or the security of home. The harder the water rushed down, the more I cried. For a moment, I gazed up at the ceiling trying to look to heaven for God to save me from this nightmare.

"God, why are you letting this happen to me?"

Hysterically stomping and kicking, I tore the shower curtain down. With rage in place of sorrow, I dropped to my knees. All the commotion made Ms. Jackson run in. I thought she was going to chastise me, but instead she got right in the shower with me and held me close.

"Get it all out baby," she coaxed. "Get it out."

Through blurry eyes, I saw my sister watching me. Hand over her mouth. Tears streaming down her cheeks. Regret in her eyes. There was proof in the saying that we never know what the day will bring. I woke up that day a little girl who was excited about the first day of school. Yet, I'd go to sleep that night as a young woman fighting for her life.

Three days turned into three weeks. Emergency youth shelters typically don't allow the kids in protective custody to go to school. Since Andrea was a senior, they made an exception for her so that she didn't get behind in her work. She routinely made it back to the shelter right before dinner, but lately, she was returning later and later.

I started my day going about the usual shelter schedule. Wake up at seven, shower, dress, and then go eat. Breakfast was always Fruit Loops out of white Styrofoam bowls or plain unsalted lumpy grits. Not having much of an appetite anyway, the poor food options made it easy to skip breakfast. Television time was amusing because nobody really watched it. The girls and boys were all too busy flirting back and forth and kissing each other every chance they got. Having no interest in their activities, I sat on the other side of the room, alone. I didn't want to talk to, much less, sit by or kiss any boys. However, it seemed a few boys had other plans for me.

Recess was the only part of the day I anticipated. It reminded me of our swing set back home. I missed playing with my brother and hearing him giggle as I pushed him on the swings. I missed sitting in the grass writing in my journal. As I sat daydreaming about my life before all this drama, the feeling of intense stares interrupted my flight from reality. Some of the older boys were watching me. Their lustful glares made me uncomfortable. Before I could get up, they were approaching me. The leader of the group gave me the creeps. His name was Quentin.

At fifteen, he was tall for his age. Although I couldn't be certain, he seemed well over six feet. He wasn't bad looking, with his brown skin and lanky physique. However, he had a pervert appeal, like the kind of stalker who peeps through your bedroom window in the dark of night. Fight or flight instincts made my heart beat fast as they got closer. Do I run or play it cool? Fear forced me to play it cool.

"Aye girl, why you don't never play with nobody?" asked Quentin.

I shrugged my shoulders, not really knowing what to say.

One of his friends chimed in, "Dang, do you talk?"

I was so afraid of what they might do that I couldn't bring my lips to part for any response to come out.

"Well, since you don't talk with that mouth, do you suck dick with it?"

The two other boys laughed hysterically. I, on the other hand, didn't know what Quentin meant. I was only ten and no one around me talked like that. Before I knew what was happening, one of the boys grabbed me and placed his hand over my mouth.

"Take her to the bushes," Quentin ordered while staring at me with his menacing eyes. "You're gonna suck my dick!"

Terror filled my mind as I watched him pull his penis out just over the top of his gray sweatpants. I began to pray to myself. "God help me."

Realizing that kicking was not working, I made my body go limp which resulted in them dropping me to the ground. Quentin used this opportunity to go in for the kill. Just as he crouched over me, with all the force my frail little body could muster, I raised my leg kneeing him in his tiny sweaty balls. This gave me just enough time to get up and run. Had I moved like that in field day, I would have easily won first place.

The chase was on. Determined to not to let them gain ground, I turned back around to speed up and slammed right into my sister. Thankfully, she didn't have work-study and decided not to go to her boyfriend Tyrone's house on this particular day. God's ***grace*** - I called on the Lord and he sent help.

"What's wrong?" she asked.

Chest heaving from running so hard, I told her everything. In less than two seconds, Andrea's face morphed into Sophia when Harpo was beating on her in *The Color Purple*. She was out for blood.

"Show me where they are," she demanded as she grabbed my hand and strutted along.

I spotted them at the basketball court pretending they'd been there the whole time. Stomping hard across the grass like an army soldier, Andrea marched right onto middle court, grabbed the basketball, and tossed it into nearby bushes.

"Which one of y'all punks messing with my sister?"

Silence. Quentin fidgeted and gave himself away. She had to leap to reach him but by the time her feet hit the ground she'd wrapped a fistful of his collar in her left hand. Simultaneously winding up her right hand like Mike Tyson, she commenced to whacking him so hard you could hear her knuckles cracking against his skull each time she connected. He begged for mercy. A crowd had formed around us and she dropped Quentin right on the middle of the court.

Andrea addressed the crowd. "Let me make this clear and I'm only saying it once. This little girl right here is my sister. Nobody, and I mean nobody, better lay a hand on her."

I didn't have any more issues with anybody messing with me after that. Throughout the ordeal, I learned a crucial lesson: Don't be afraid to yell for your life and always be willing to fight. God's ***grace*** had covered me, but the lesson had hardened me. Shortly after the Quentin ordeal, Ms. Dillan arrived with a message. "You have a visit scheduled with your mom today."

I hadn't seen Mama and Daddy in over a month. I thought I was still dreaming when the case worker told me I'd finally get to visit with them. However, I immediately felt sick when I caught sight of the DFACS building. That was the place where I was taken from my mom so it was ironic that I had to go back here to visit her. Mama was already there waiting for me, and I instantly burst into tears when I saw her face. Inhaling her embrace, she still smelled like Keri lotion mixed with cigarettes, I longed to stay right there in her arms.

Mama was upset by my weight loss and begged me to eat. Talking a million words per minute, I explained why I wasn't eating and told her about my shelter attack. The more I spoke of my misadventures, the angrier she got. When the visit was over, she told me she loved me, and I heard her tell Ms. Dillan that she needed to speak to her. The visit went by so quickly that I didn't even get a chance to find out why Daddy wasn't there.

By the time I arrived at the shelter, it was dinnertime and Andrea wasn't there. I ate a little applesauce just to please Mama. After saying my prayers, I drifted off to sleep but was jarred awake from piercing screams. Quentin tried to kill himself with a razor blade. He was found lying on his cot in a pool of blood. I'd never seen that much blood in my life. I had to get out of there. So, guess what? I prayed.

When I woke up the next morning, Andrea still hadn't made it back to the shelter. Her newfound freedom was unfair. How could she leave me in the shelter alone? All of this was her doing, yet I was the one stuck.

I called Ms. Dillan to deliver the bad news about Quentin only to find out she had good news for me. "I'm on my way to pick you up. You're leaving the shelter."

My prayers were answered. I was finally going home. But just as fast as I felt joy, sorrow quickly replaced it when Ms. Dillan finished her statement.

"I found a foster home that has room for both you and your sister."

"Wait! I'm not going home?" I asked.

"Oh no dear, you're not. But this place will be a lot better than the shelter. You'll at least have a room and a bed."

Ms. Dillan

Overworked and underpaid. Your job was to advocate for the weak and voiceless children placed in your care. Instead you were an advocate for your caseload making it impossible to see that compassion was the one thing I needed from you the most.

Sometimes good intentions aren't good enough. I was just one of a million cases she'd work which was evident through her lack of attachment and genuine empathy for my situation. If only she'd shut her mouth and listen, she could see that I wasn't just some orphan. I had a family. I didn't need a caseworker, I needed someone to have empathy.

Romans 15:1 "Now we who are strong ought to bear the weaknesses of those without strength, not just please ourselves..."

Ms. Dillan had allowed her job to desensitize her to listening to the children she was charged with protecting. Her piles of paperwork were her only focus. Closing the case and closing the file was all she cared about. She was too busy rushing along she couldn't hear me.

My spirit had been broken because as a child I was unprotected. No one listened to me when I cried out. Now as a mother, I've learned to listen more and speak less. At one time, this was the hardest thing for me to do. I thought chastising was teaching them, but now I realize shutting my mouth enables me to be in tune to what they're feeling and be sensitive to them when they make mistakes. I can more easily identify when and why they need help. Shutting my mouth has helped me savor the sounds of their voices and share their joy when I hear their laughter. When my mouth is silent, I can sense when they're afraid, nervous, worried, or anxious. Shutting my mouth has given me guidance on what to pray for involving their day to day lives, dreams, hopes, and their walk with God. Shutting my mouth has opened my eyes to see them for who they are and get a peek inside their hearts to see who they're going to be. The best part about shutting my mouth is that I found out just how much wisdom they have and that they are learning what I've been trying so hard to teach them.

These were all the things Ms. Dillan would have learned about me had she only shut her mouth and listened.

CHAPTER 6

I didn't care about a room. I wanted my room and my bed. But, once again, I didn't have a say-so. I had a mouth and I could speak, but I had no voice. I was powerless.

Pulling up to the dark brown, split-level house, I noticed Andrea was already there parked at the curb with her boyfriend, Tyrone. Seeing her get out of her boyfriend's car sporting brand new clothes, I began to question her motives in all of this. She was different. She was hiding something from me. Besides, I assumed we were in this together, but I was the only one feeling like a prison inmate. Slowly, I got out of the car clinging to a bag filled with a few toiletries that Ms. Jackson, the nice lady from the shelter, had given me. Ms. Dillan was in a hurry so she walked ahead of us. Before she could ring the bell, a heavy-set woman with a dry, salt-and-pepper colored Jheri Curl opened the door. I tried not to stare but that hair hadn't seen a drop of activator in months. She looked tired and irritated, like we had interrupted her from a nap, but she did manage to introduce herself.

"Hey, I'm Ms. Benjamin."

Ms. Dillan greeted her but only took one step inside. Standing less than an inch in the doorway, she reached in her purse and pulled out two envelopes. "These are vouchers to J. C. Penny. You both have one hundred dollars to spend. Spend it wisely. You all need school clothes."

She gave us four tokens to ride the Marta bus to the mall the next day. She didn't bother to see to it that we got settled in before she was out the door – presumably to work on a different case. Wondering if things could get any worse, I began to cry. Ms. Benjamin didn't flinch. She looked at my sister and said, "Let me show y'all to where you're gonna sleep."

Our bedroom was downstairs in a dark, mildew-smelling basement. We placed our few belongings on the bed and went back upstairs for dinner. We met the other foster kids who lived in the home. Two of the children were Ms. Benjamin's twin granddaughters who were about my age. Their names were Jubilee and Janay. Double trouble if you ask me. Completing the roster of siblings was a toddler named Robert, Benson who was a preteen, and Jason, Ms. Benjamin's mentally disabled son. He was nearly thirty but had the mind of a child.

I had no appetite and by the looks of the one pot mixture which contained boiled chicken, collard greens, mashed black eyed peas, and cornbread, skipping a meal was going to be easy. After dinner, I went back to our mildew-scented room and cried myself to sleep. The next day we rode the Marta bus to South DeKalb Mall. With Mama we didn't shop at the mall much except for maybe around Easter so this was a treat. Otherwise, we shopped at Richway, a popular discount department store in our neighborhood.

For a moment, I was smiling and enjoying myself. That is, until we saw how little a hundred bucks can buy at the mall. I chose a pair of jeans that had pink stars on the pockets but Andrea convinced me to get something that wasn't so noticeable because I'dhave to wear them every day. Done shopping, we caught the Marta bus back to the foster home. I ended up walking most of the way alone because my sister stayed at the bus stop to catch the next bus to Tyrone's house.

Once I got to the foster home, I went straight to my room and wrote in my journal until dinner time, when Ms. Benjamin called me upstairs. Having no plans to eat, I silent sat as she served the same nauseating one-pot concoction of a meal. My thoughts of vomiting at the sight of the food were interrupted when Ms. Benjamin informed me I'd be starting school Monday.

On the first day of school at Tilson Elementary, a friendly girl named Nikki approached me right after the dismissal bell. "Hey, you're the new foster girl at Ms. Benjamin's house, aren't you?"

Hearing the words foster girl made me ashamed so I answered slowly. "Yes, how do you know that?"

"I live across the street and saw you get out of the car the other day."

Still digesting my new label as foster girl, I wanted to run off and hide my embarrassment but Nikki kept on with the conversation.

"You're very pretty. You don't look like a foster girl."

"Thanks, you're pretty too," I said. "Oh yeah, I'm not really a foster girl. I have a Mama and a Daddy."

Nikki took the cue and dropped the conversation. I didn't hold it against her though. There was something about her warm personality that made me comfortable. I knew I could consider her a friend.

Nikki and I began meeting up every morning to walk to school together. She introduced me to her mom, Mrs. Michaels. I could see where she got her good looks. Her mother could've past for Tina Knowles's twin sister. Mrs. Michaels gregarious personality jumped right out at me. Upon meeting, her first words were, "Chile are you eating?"

I didn't realize my once chubby body had turned to skin and bones. "I only eat applesauce at school," I responded, solemnly.

Taking pity on me, she invited me in for breakfast and told me I could also stop by on the way home from school to eat dinner. "We're having spaghetti tonight. Come over and make sure you eat, baby."

I couldn't wait to take her up on her offer. Months had gone by without a decent meal, so the thought of spaghetti made my mouth water. It was an early dinner, that would surely leave me hungry again before the night was through, but it was more than I had been eating so I couldn't complain. Once again God's ***grace*** covered me.

I'd been eating breakfast and lunch every day for two weeks and had gotten comfortable with being around their family. One morning, while eating, I felt Mrs. Michaels gazing closely at me. "Baby, do you have clothes?"

Shame crept over me again and I uttered, "The few clothes I had were stolen by Ms. Benjamin's granddaughters."

On my first week in the foster home, I'd come home from school to find the Double Mint Twins outside riding bikes in my new clothes. They had even stolen my panties. Andrea put a lock on our door to keep them out of our room when we were gone but that didn't bring back the clothes they had already taken. Hearing my story, Mrs. Michaels shed a few tears before sharing with me a solution. "Well how about this, can you leave ten minutes earlier each morning?"

Through my tears, I responded, "Yes, Ms. Benjamin doesn't care what I do."

"Good. I'll have an outfit for you to wear to school every day. You'll change clothes over here before you go to school and switch back after school."

In between sobs, I thanked Mrs. Michaels, but I also thanked God.

Andrea enjoyed even more freedom living in the foster home. No parental supervision. No curfew. She'd leave early in the morning for school and didn't come back until late at night, if she made it back at all. The first few nights she left me alone I was petrified, but the lock on the door gave me a little peace of mind. I should've known my sense of security wouldn't last – especially with my luck or lack thereof.

Jason, Ms. Benjamin's mute son seemed harmless on first impression. Usually, he'd sit in the living room all day making weird noises. He'd hum loudly, "Yum-------Yum -------- Yum."

His mumble jumble scared me but what was more frightening was how excited he seemed to get when he saw me. His eyes would buck, he'd grab his private, and instead of making the yum-yum sound, he'd moan. I avoided him as much as possible and made sure to use the restroom before he came downstairs for the night. This seemed to work for the most part but when my sister didn't come home one night, I broke my normal routine and left the room looking for her.

With my mind still foggy from sleep, I forgot about Jason and headed straight to the kitchen to search for Andrea. Just as I made it to the stairs, Jason was sitting there, butt naked dead smack in the middle of the landing. We were face to face. What was I going to do? He grinned at me, but his eyes were dark. Although he couldn't speak, his salivating tongue said it all. He wanted me in the worst way. Slowly, I stepped backwards trying to make it back to my room. Once I had gotten my footing, I took off running but wasn't fast enough. Swooping me off ground, he headed in the direction of his room. I couldn't let that happen. Tears flooding my eyes, my mind raced with questions: Where was Andrea? Where was Mama? Where was Daddy? Weren't they supposed to protect me? But only God could help me.

Then, a line from ***Psalm 23*** popped in my head. It was a verse that Mama prayed all the time. Speaking it aloud, I found my strength. "Ye, though I walk through the valley of the shadow of death. I will fear no evil for you are with me."

Tossing me on the bed like a ragdoll, he pinned me down. Being around the older kids at the shelter, I had a good idea of what was next. Refusing to be a victim, I waited for him to come close enough to grab his penis. He was going to learn his lesson if it was the last thing I did. I dug my nails into the sides of his penis and squeezed as hard as I could. I wanted to tear it off from its base. No yum-yum sound this time, he was moaning in pure agony. His whimpering was so ear-splitting that I thought he'd wake up the whole neighborhood. I wanted to make him pay. Finally, I saw a light come on in the hallway. It was Ms. Benjamin. She begged me to release my grip. It took a while before I snapped back into reality. As I let go, I thought again, why me Lord?

I didn't tell anyone what happened with Jason. Andrea hadn't been home, and besides, she might've killed him. Therefore, I kept my mouth shut because I definitely didn't need things to get worse. Ms. Benjamin didn't allow me to use the phone, and in fact, unplugged them all from the wall so I couldn't call anyone. I'd made my point to Jason, though, and I was certain, he'd never try me again. God had protected me. I went on about my days and held the secret inside.

Spoiled collard greens, boiled chicken, and rice was the nightly foster home dinner menu. Except for me, every child in the house had constant diarrhea. Knowing their stomach aches came from the spoiled food she cooked, Ms. Benjamin served Pepto Bismol as dessert. Prison meals weren't for me, so I never ate. Instead, I'd sit in the kitchen long enough to listen to her rant.

"You think you high and mighty like you too good to eat." More insults followed her nasty remarks. "Little girl you may as well get off your high horse and realize you ain't no better than the rest of us. You ain't nothing but a foster child, like all of 'em. This gonna be your life, like it or not."

Staring at the bowl each night, I'd sit there and wouldn't eat a thing. My refusal to devour the pile of garbage she made the kids eat, also represented my refusal to accept the words she was saying to me. This was not my life and it was not my fate.

However, Ms. Benjamin was determined to get a victory under her belt. Placing the usual bowl of chicken and rice slop in front of me, she glared at me with hateful eyes. Not realizing she was watching me, I crinkled my face at the food, and before I knew it, I was staring at the end of a wooden spatula. The spatula was so close to my face I had to push back from the table to focus. Ms. Benjamin was glaring at me with so much anger and hatred I thought she was going to hit me with it.

"You turning your face up at my food," she said. "I ought to hit you in the nose right now and force you to eat it so you will know what happens when you turn your nose up at something."

Memories of being force fed by my grandmother ran through my mind before I rose from the table and made a formal declaration. "You hit me with that spoon, you better kill me, 'cause if you let me live, you won't see tomorrow. Don't nobody hit me in my face."

I slapped the spoon out of my face, and then did a forearm sweep to slap the bowl clear across the table. I'd had it. "And another thing, that food is sour. That's why everybody in this house stays sick at the stomach."

Once I had finally spoken my peace, I purposely brushed past her and went to my room.

Angry thoughts were my lullaby as I fell into a deep sleep until my bladder felt as though it was about to explode. I had to pee, and there was no way I could hold it until morning. Unfortunately, I forgot to go before Jason came down to bed for the night. Peeping out and seeing that his light was off, I raced down the hall to the bathroom. I was so relieved to finally go, that I forgot to make sure the coast was clear before heading back to my room. As I darted out, I bumped right into Jason who was standing beside my bedroom door. Again, he was butt naked with his hand on the door knob to my room. He didn't hear me at first. Fear paralyzed me as I flashed back to our last encounter. Why was he standing outside my door? Did he do this often? When he turned around and I saw his eyes, my train of thought broke immediately. Those same dark eyes I'd seen before, only this time, they were telling me he'd get what he wanted.

The fighter in me finally woke up and I didn't intend to run anymore. He was going to move out of my way. With all rational thinking out the window, I walked up to him so he could hear me loud and clear. Pointing my finger directly in his face, I said "If you don't move out my way, I'm going to rip that little dick of yours off this time."

He might have been a mute but there was nothing wrong with his eyes and ears. Amid our face off, I heard keys jingling in the lock at the front door upstairs. Knowing it was Andrea, I got even bolder and shoved him out of my way. As I closed the door behind me, I saw him rush back to his room. Andrea unknowingly saved me that night but what would happen the next time?

My problems were only multiplying because the limited protection Andrea provided was running out. She was turning eighteen in few weeks and would be aging out of the system. This meant she'd move out of the foster home and I'd be left there alone, totally unprotected. That's when I realized it was never too early to start praying for an escape route.

Ms. Benjamin's House

House of horrors. House of dread. Depression lived within the walls of that place.

The scent of old chicken grease, dirty carpet, and mothballs burned my nose. Ms. Benjamin's house was pure misery. I hated every moment of my time confined within her abode. It was a dungeon of doom. Every day after school, when I walked back inside, it was like entering a dark gray prison of despair. Mostly, Ms. Benjamin wore a house robe nearly throughout the day. Always mean, angry, snappy, and frustrated. She hated her life and didn't try to hide it. There was never much light in that house or maybe there was so much hurt, pain, and problems that it clouded and blocked what little light might have been there. She never opened the curtains, either, so that didn't help.

I would walk in afterschool and her granddaughters would be running amuck. She would scream at them and make all sorts of idle threats. When I look back, I believe she resented having to raise her grandkids. Every once in awhile, their mother would stop by. She would bring them a piece of candy, quickly shew them away, and then get to the reason for her visit, which was to ask for money. Ms. Benjamin would reach into her bra, give her some money, tell her she needs to come get her 'chil-len' and before she could get another word out, her daughter would be out the door.

Philippians 4:11-12 "For I have learned how to be content with whatever I have. I know how to live on almost nothing or with everything..."

Life had been filled with hundreds of situations and circumstances that I'd no control over, but the one thing I could control was my mouth AND the way I viewed my surroundings. There was good in every situation and every situation would eventually work out. One of the benefits of contentment is that you open the gateways for blessings to come to you. When I divorced my first husband, I decided to let him have the house. I was happy in my apartment and God would provide me with another house when it was time. Also, allowing my ex-husband to keep the house instead of selling it and splitting the profits, meant my children could hold onto something familiar and stay in their same schools. I knew it was important for them to have stability. Besides, God had given me joy and I was not about to risk losing it over a house.

A little sprucing was all my apartment needed. No, it wasn't the five-bedroom home that I'd grown to adore but it would be my new Queendom.

Decorating the boys' room and bathroom lifted all our spirits. Adding a couple of bar stools transformed the kitchen into the perfect breakfast nook. A dining table and large area rug gave us a new formal dining area and we could eat dinner as a family. Vases and framed inspirational quotes gave our living room personality and a white bistro set placed in the corner of my balcony gave me the sweetest spot for drinking coffee or wine as I journaled. Little touches of roses and candles made it cozy and inviting. I had joy, and I poured it into my little apartment.

Ms. Benjamin's house was just a building made of brick, walls and a ceiling. The despair rose from the floor to the rooftop. I promised myself that I would never live in a house like that again. From that experience, I learned how to ensure my dwelling was always a home full of love and light. Oh, and I cooked with a dash of love – my boys have never eaten boiled chicken slop.

CHAPTER 7

The next morning, I awoke to banging on the door. It was Ms. Benjamin yelling, "Your caseworker just called, and she gonna pick you up from school so you can see ya Mama today."

"Ok," I responded through the door. I kept my excitement to a minimum out of fear that she'd steal my happiness away if she saw even a glimpse of it.

"And take that damn lock off the door in my house before I take the damn hinges off."

Though I was happy I'd see my mom, the feeling haunted me. Happiness always came right before I found myself in another jam. Worry settled in about my visit. Should

I tell Mama what Andrea had been doing? Or, should I just keep my mouth shut?

Like waiting for paint to dry, school dismissal took forever. Timing my feet with the bell, I dashed outside to Ms. Dillan's car. My goal was to get to Mama as fast as possible. As we rode to our meeting spot, I kept daydreaming that someone would save me. Perhaps, somebody powerful would walk in and say, "Kira you can go home."

For a minute, I thought my daydream had come true when I entered the waiting room and saw it filled with various family members. Scanning the room for Mama, I spotted her rushing toward me. Ms. Dillan briefly intercepted our paths. "Only two visitors at a time and y'all have 30 minutes."

Virtually knocking Ms. Dillan out of the way, I hugged Mama. Inhaling that Keri lotion and cigarette smell caused me to realize how much I missed her signature scent. Eager to catch Mama up on all that had been happening, I started talking before we made it to the visitation room. Mama squeezed my hand indicating for me to shut up and wait for us to be alone. Once the door was shut, I ran my mouth like a waterfall flowing over the side of a cliff.

"Mama, Andrea staying out all night with her boyfriend. Some nights she doesn't come home. My clothes were stolen. The food in the foster home is sour. I'm not eating it."

Mama sat silent, letting me get it all out.

"One more thing, Mama. They think Daddy touched me when he didn't."

I felt the tears creeping up in my eyes. We didn't have much time left before we had to share it with the rest of the family, so Mama kept her words short. "Kira, listen. Calm down. Remember the Serenity Prayer I taught you?"

"Yes, Mama."

"Let's say it together."

In unison, we prayed. "God grant me the serenity to accept the things I cannot change, the courage to change the things I can, and the wisdom to know the difference between the two."

Before that day, I'd memorized the prayer only because it hung on the wall in the bathroom so I'd see it every time I used the toilet. Finally, though, I understood what the prayer meant. The prayer was about the POWER OF WORDS, using them to gain strength and courage for whatever battle was ahead. Mama told me two more things before our time was up. "I'm going to see to it that I you get your clothes and shoes. I'll send them in your favorite Rainbow Brite suitcase."

I felt a little better until she hit me with her next words. "Kira, you're going to testify in court about your Daddy. Don't be afraid of testifying. Simply tell the truth. Your words have power. Use them. The truth will always set you free."

To this day, I carry those words close to my heart.

For the next twenty minutes, my family members rotated in and out. The last duo to visit me was my Great-Aunt Elsie, my grandfather's sister on my mom's side, and her daughter, Vicki, my older cousin by fourteen years. She was the cool cousin we all looked up to and wanted to emulate. Since her and Andrea were around the same age, they hung out often, but whenever she visited, she always made time for me. As an only child, she loved hanging out with us because we felt like her little sisters. Aunt Elsie on the other hand was somewhat the politician of the family. Everything she did was to gain recognition as our family's oldest living matriarch. Her visit was merely a duty but I knew Vicki persuaded her to come. Either way, I was glad they came.

Before I knew it, the visit was over. Ms. Dillan and I walked back through the lobby together. Quickly, I told everyone goodbye and hugged Mama one last time. During our embrace, Mama whispered, "Serenity and truth."

Something was up. Instead of doing her usual drop and roll after my visits, Ms. Dillan walked me inside. For once, Andrea was home when I called her name. We both sat down in the greasy kitchen while Ms. Dillan explained the reason for coming in.

"On Monday, you girls will meet the prosecutor to prepare for trial," she blurted matter-of-factly. "Kira, I'll be back in a couple of days because your mother wants to send you some clothes."

After she left, I went to take a shower. While drying off, I heard what sounded like crying. It was Andrea. I cracked the door open so I could hear. She was on the phone with our mom. Up until that point, we weren't allowed to call home and all the phones had been removed so I didn't know how she got the opportunity to call. Anyway, I kept listening.

Andrea was speaking in between sobs. "Mama, I can't tell them the truth now. It's too late. They'll put me in jail if I do."

I didn't know what Mama was saying on the other end but Andrea's next words floored me. "Grandma Helen told me to say it. She said it would get me out of the house so I could come live with her. I didn't know they would take Kira too."

When I heard her stomping down the hall after hanging up, I sprang to attention. Like a mad woman, she burst through the door with fiery red eyes.

"I called mom to ask her to send me some of my clothes too, and guess what?"

"I don't feel like playing guessing games," I said. "Spit it out."

"You ratted me out! Why'd you tell her I wasn't coming home and was staying out late?"

"Yeah, I told her. So what? You 've been leaving me here by myself in this hell hole. And you'd better be glad I didn't tell her about Rick."

Rick was Nikki's older brother and she'd told me that Andrea and Rick got caught having sex by Mrs. Michaels.

"You better watch your mouth, little girl. I can still kick your butt." Andrea was ready to fight, but I was too.

Not only was I angry because she had the audacity to confront me, after all she'd been doing, but she and my Grandma Helen had told a lie. A lie that ripped our family to bits.

"You and Grandma Helen have schemed and ripped our family into a thousand pieces. And for what? So you can run wild and she can get revenge on Daddy?"

Before I knew it, I felt a sting go across my face. Andrea literally slapped the taste out of my mouth. I don't know what got into me but I slapped her right back. The fight was on. Punching, snatching, grabbing, kicking, and slapping. We were tearing the room up. Ms. Benjamin must have heard the ruckus because she burst in and got between us. She warned us to stop or she'd call the police. I ran outside. I didn't know how to get home but that's where I was heading. Andrea ran out behind me. Fists up and ready for round two, I quickly turned around. Instead of throwing a punch at me, Andrea hugged me. We both burst into tears while standing in the middle of the street. Once we pulled ourselves together, we walked back into the driveway.

Andrea apologized first. "I'm sorry, sis. I love you and let's promise to never fight each other again."

The stress had taken a toll on both of us and we unleashed on each other.

"Why'd you do it? Why'd you lie?" I asked.

"I wanted to escape all the responsibility Mama placed on me. She's always made me take care of you, Kyle, the house, everything. Meanwhile, she ran after Daniel and every man before that. I never meant to bring you into this."

"Can't you just tell the truth and make it all go away?"

"No, it's too late for that. They'll take me to jail. And they'll take Grandma Helen too. I can't do that to her."

I was at a loss of words, so I sat there silently thinking to myself: *But what about me? How could she have done this to me?*

The Family Unit

The family that prays together stays together.

Striving to be different than my parents, whose marriage was left vulnerable to attacks, I had to think and act differently. Their marriage wasn't grounded in prayer. They weren't a unified team living by God's word. Therefore, numerous outside distractions prevented them from focusing on God's word. I had to dig deeper.

Matthew 7:24 - "Everyone then who hears these words of mine and does them will be like a wise man who built his house on the rock..."

With the divorce rate higher than fifty percent, it's obvious marriage is under attack. Therefore, we must pray and devote time to God individually and as couples. The devil doesn't want to see unions thrive but it's not just the devil attacking marriage. Yes, the devil knows that when two gather together and declare anything on Earth it shall be done but he's no longer worried about that because couples aren't gathering together. The image and value of marriage has been diluted by many of the unhealthy examples we're exposed to today. When celebrities call it quits, the demise of their union and destruction of their family is glamorized and glorified at divorce parties. Everyone seems to be getting out of a bad marriage or deciding not to get into one altogether. By the droves, women are settling to act like wives but without the title and without the blessings that come with it. Why? Because marriage is hard and selfishness makes us not want to work when it gets difficult. It's easier to run away and retreat, start over with someone new, or pretend we're okay being forever girlfriends or being by ourselves. I'm guilty as charged.

Somewhere along the line, I realized I wanted better. I knew my value. I loved my independence and freedom but

God created me to share my gifts with others – especially with a husband. As I journaled, I discovered the answer to divorce wasn't just having a prayer life but having a prayer life with my mate. Immense power comes from the prayers of both the husband and wife together. That power is the building block for the family unit.

My husband and I are accomplishing great things together through our prayers. God's word is the foundation on which our marriage is built. Storms will come that might make our union weeble and wobble. Perhaps we'll endure a few cracks, but built on God's foundation, our family won't crumble.

CHAPTER 8

Ms. Benjamin's home wasn't the only place I feared. New hells were popping up daily. Places the old me, the one who once lived in a loving home with a family, never knew existed. So, you could imagine my horror when I was forced to visit a psychiatrist. Entering his office had me shaking like a leaf in a wind tunnel. My initial anxiety disappeared when I was greeted by a man who looked exactly like Mr. Rogers from the PBS children's show. I did a double take to make sure my eyes weren't playing tricks on me.

While extending his hand, he said, "I'm Dr. Glen. Nice to meet you Kira."

Hesitantly, I leaned back into the chair nearest his desk. He sat down and crossed his legs. As he pulled out a writing tablet, he asked, "Do you know why you're here today?"

"No sir, I don't."

"I'll be evaluating you to see if you've suffered any trauma."

"What does trauma mean?" I'd never heard that word before but I knew it didn't sound to appealing.

"Trauma is a deeply distressing experience." He eased into the session by showing me a series of basic pictures. My job was to say the first thing that came to mind.

"Apple. Dog. Tree." Seemed pretty simple.

But then he showed me an abstract picture that looked like spilled paint and I had no idea what to say out of my mouth. I paused, taking it all in.

Then, he asked, "What comes to mind?"

"I don't know." My shoulders shrugged in confusion. "Spilled paint?"

He went to the next card and asked me again. "What comes to mind?"

It too looked like spilled paint, so I repeated my description. He kept flipping card after card. To me, they all looked like spilled paint. Digging further into the pile, he flipped over a card that looked different.

"Butterfly," I said.

As the cards finished, he rose from his chair and motioned toward the door. "Let's take a visit to the toy area."

The room was colorfully decorated and had lots of books with toys set up in different corners. It reminded me of my third grade classroom. Dolls scattered on the table seemed out of place and instantly gave me an eerie feeling. Cautiously following his instructions to make myself comfortable, I sat down on the floor next to the table. As I eyeballed the dolls, I noticed the male doll wasn't made like my Ken doll. He had a penis. I thought to myself: *I'm not playing with that doll, something isn't right with it.*

As I examined the female doll more closely, I noticed she too had real-looking body parts and didn't resemble my Barbie at all. So, I opted to just sit still. I was maturing quickly, beyond that of an average ten-year-old, and wisdom told me that if I played with anything in that room they'd say I was traumatized. Hence, I resolved to just sit there for what seemed like forever.

Basically, I was in a standoff with the dolls until Dr. Glen interrupted our silent war. "How'd you like playing with the dolls?"

"I didn't play with them," I quickly responded.

"Why not?"

I picked one up and stared at it. "They don't look like toys."

"What do you mean?"

"They don't look like Barbie and Ken." I wanted to just say **DUH** but I figured that'd be rude.

He took a seat next to me. "How about we play a game?" Holding both dolls up, he asked, "Can you point to the boy doll?"

I pointed to the boy doll.

"How do you know it's a boy doll?"

Feeling like this was a trap, I answered his question with a question. "Do you know which one is a boy doll?"

"Yes, I do."

"Well, how do you know which one is a boy?"

Caught off guard by my answer, he moved on. "Can you point out the girl doll?"

I pointed to the girl doll.

"How do you know it's a girl doll?"

Once again, I knew not to answer his question, so I quizzed him back. "Do you know which one is a girl doll?"

"Yes, I do."

"Well how do you know which one is a girl?"

I'd hoped my answers would irritate him enough to stop asking me questions, but he placed the boy doll on top of the girl doll and went on with his questions.

"Do you know what game the dolls are playing?"

"Yeah I do," I snapped. "They are playing the game the teenagers in the shelter played with each other."

Getting under his skin was my goal. I'd make sure he knew that instead of my parents traumatizing me, I'd been traumatized by everything I'd gone through since being taken away from home. That session birthed my smart-mouth defense mechanism. Wittiness had shown its face.

Suddenly, Dr. Glen wasn't as friendly as Mr. Rogers. Contrarily, he had become quite curt and began to chastise me. "Kira, you're a bright girl and I believe you know more than what you say to me. Are you holding anything back?"

He'd struck a nerve that unleashed the monster inside of me who was forced to grow up too soon. Fear and politeness went out the window. I rose from the floor so that I could speak my mind concisely. Tell my truth. Fight for myself.

A voice much older than mine, one I didn't recognize, rose from my throat. "Dr. Glen, you're not going to make me say anything that's not true. You can move those dolls in any direction you want, but it won't change the truth."

Watching him write feverishly on his tablet enraged me more. "Here is what you can write on your tablet," I said. "The only trauma I have is from being taken away from my parents. If you don't plan to help get me back home, you're wasting my time!"

Surprisingly, Dr. Glen agreed with me. "Kira, you're much wiser than your age. You are correct, we are wasting time. I've made my conclusion. I'll submit my report to the judge first thing Monday morning. You have severe trauma."

As he said those words, I felt like Florida Evans on *Good Times*. **Damn. Damn. Damn.**

My Mouth

Collateral damage from traumatizing events. Unprotected and defenseless. I used the one weapon I had, my mouth!

Before Dr. Glen's office, I never understood the power of my mouth, particularly, my words. They could work for me or against me. Good or bad, my words could help or hinder me and the outcomes of my life. Both held enormous power but it was up to me to figure out how to use them.

Ecclesiastes 3:7 "A time to tear and a time to mend. A time to be silent and a time to speak…"

Even with my mouth issues and all the tests that I have failed because of it, I never cease to pray. I do everything I can to learn from my failures and continue using God's word. My first marriage failed, not solely because of my mouth but I used my tongue as a weapon and did not use it the way God intended. When I realized that God had saw fit to give me a second chance and send me to the man he had chosen for me, I made a vow to not let my mouth blow it. But don't think I get it right all the time. It's taken countless prayers for this mouth of mine and wisdom that I've learned over the years to make me the wife I am today. I'm still a work in progress and I'm sure my wonderful husband will attest to that. Fortunately, my mouth is nowhere near where it was when we married and even further from the way it was when he met me.

God restored the stability, security, foundation, and family that I had been missing for almost twenty-five years. I was reaping my harvest. It was not God's intention for me to feel helpless, weak, trapped and full of regret. He wanted me to be strong, full of wisdom – knowing when to speak and when to be silent.

CHAPTER 9

If things couldn't get any worse after my psychiatric evaluation, Ms. Dillan called.

"Your court date has been pushed up," she said. "Tomorrow you all will meet the prosecutor. He'll prep you for your testimony.

Confusion momentarily paralyzed my thoughts. I didn't realize that what I said to Dr. Glen would lead me to court. I thought my words were going to get me out of the foster home and back to the safety of my parents.

"What do you mean by prosecutor and testimony?" I asked. "Am I going to jail or something?"

I hadn't done anything wrong but so many ridiculous things were happening, it was possibility.

"You're not going to jail, but your father is, for molestation."

"What's molestation?"

"Your father touched you and Andrea inappropriately."

"Where'd you get that idea from? My dad never touched us inappro—"

"It's okay," she interrupted. "You don't have to protect him. He won't be able to do that to you anymore."

"BUT my dad never touched me." I yelled.

"You're just in denial. The counselor wrote in his report that your refusal to touch the dolls indicated you were protecting your father."

Deflated from hearing those words, defeat set in. My stunt at the counseling session had backfired. Was there no one I could trust? Why was no one listening to me? They were treating me like a mute button. Push to turn on when we want to hear you. Push to turn off when we don't. I was just plain tired of the mess my sister had gotten me into. Andrea was running amuck, enjoying her new life while Daddy was stuck in jail and I was stuck in hell. I knew I'd have to fight my way out of this but for the life of me, I didn't know how.

Preparation day for Daddy's trial came too quick. Waiting to get started, I was shaking uncontrollably. We were introduced to a lady with a fancy title, adjudicator something.

Andrea went first. Most of the questions were just general inquiries about her age and grade in school. Andrea would be asked to point out my father and confirm his relation to her. Relaxing a bit, I thought, maybe this won't be so bad. That is until she asked Andrea the next question.

"Have you ever witnessed your parents do drugs?"

Hearing the question made me choke on my own saliva. Why would she ask her that? What does that have to do with anything. Surely, my sister was not stupid enough to answer. Like many Black households, we had an unspoken rule in our house: *what goes on in this house, stays in this house.*

They'd have these get-togethers with their friends and us kids knew we were going to have a ton of fun because we'd have no adult supervision for hours while our parents listened to music, played Spades, drank alcohol, and did drugs. During their get-togethers, we couldn't come out of the bedroom until an adult called us or came to get us. However, we'd take turns sneaking a peek of what was going on only to be struck in the face by the strong aroma of marijuana.

Occasionally, I'd be the one summoned because I knew all the lyrics to Prince songs and they'd all be too high to remember I wasn't supposed to be out there. That's when I'd catch a glimpse of the mirrored tray with white lines of powder on them. I knew what they were doing was wrong but also knew we were never to speak of it. So, how could my sister answer that question? I know she wouldn't break the cardinal rule of every Black household.

Well, I was dead wrong. Andrea had transformed into a different person when she answered the adjudicator lady. She spoke with a vengeful tone. It was similar to Grandma Helen's.

"Yes," she admitted, "I've witnessed them doing drugs."

Because of my constant choking, which was an attempt at disrupting Andrea's testimony, I was taken to the next room. As I awaited my turn, my stomach flipped continually. Mama had said to tell the truth but I didn't want to say anything that would get them in trouble. Although they did drugs and I knew it was wrong, I still wanted to protect them. After all, they were my parents.

My turn came sooner than expected with the adjudicator lady asking me the same line of questions as my sister. "Did you ever witness your parents do drugs?"

I dropped my head and answered solemnly, "Yes."

Satisfied, she asked the next question. "Has your father ever touched you in a way that made you feel uncomfortable?"

Firmly, I quickly answered, "NO!"

Pausing, for a bit, she asked, "Has your father ever touched you in a way that he'd touch your mother?"

"I don't understand your question."

"Okay, let me ask you this. Has your father ever touched you in your private places?"

"NO!"

"Has your father ever hit you on your rear end?"

"NO!"

"Not even for a spanking?"

"Nope," I tooted my nose up in the air before continuing. "My daddy doesn't spank me."

"Let me get this straight," she said while shuffling through a pile of papers, "you're telling me that your father has never touched you inappropriately?"

"No!"

She slammed the papers on the table. "I'll be right back."

I sat in the room for a while and waited until the Assistant District Attorney entered. He'd gained recognition as being an expert prosecutor on crimes against children. He was a polite man but very direct. Speaking deliberately with every word, he questioned me about my parents' drug use then about my dad touching me. I gave him the same answers as I did to the adjudicator. He then asked for my sister to be brought in.

"Our case is built on the fact that you both were molested," he explained.

If only I could shut my mouth, I wouldn't have asked my next question. "Who told you that? My daddy never touched me or my sister."

Keeping a composed facial expression, he looked directly at my sister and then back to me. "Your sister told us. You don't have to hide it anymore. That's why we're here, to protect you and to keep your father from ever doing this again."

"But he didn't do anything," I exclaimed.

"Don't be afraid. We can put him away for a really long time and you'll both be safe."

No matter how many times I denied it, nobody was listening to me. Or maybe they just didn't believe me. I couldn't understand what was going on. Wisdom forced me to keep my mouth shut until I could figure out how to get out of this pickle. For the rest of the interview, I listened as they told me what I was going to say on the stand.

With disbelief, I watched Andrea go along with everything. I didn't recognize her. She deserved an Academy Award for her performance. She willingly went along with their little game using the key words: uncomfortable, afraid, scared. I repeated my coerced statements. Bubbling inside with anger, it took everything to keep my mouth shut, but I needed time to come up with a plan.

The night before the trial, Andrea was gone again. I couldn't sleep a wink as I tossed and turned, replaying everything over in my mind. Then, something moved inside me and I felt like I needed to pray to God:

Lord, you are my shepherd and I know I shall not want but I want and need you to save me. Fix it so I don't have to testify. Make the car break down so we miss court. Lord, I'm afraid. I don't know what to do. They want me to make stuff up on my daddy and I can't do that. You have to save me.

A stream of tears ran down my face. Tears for Daddy. Tears for Mama. Tears for Kyle. Tears for the happy family we once had.

Trial day had come much quicker than anticipated. Pulling out the Rainbow Brite suitcase that Mama had sent, I hugged it tightly to my chest. It reminded me of being back home and waking up in my room. It was the only fragment of my former life that I had left. I could still smell the clothesline scent on my clothes. Washing them would've made them lose their familiar smell so I tried my best not to wear anything she packed. However, since this was a special occasion, I pulled out a white sweater and black corduroy pants.

Andrea finally made it back to the foster home and we didn't say one word to each other. Part of me loved her because she was my big sister and was supposed to be my first best friend. Yet another part of me hated her. She was my villain, my first enemy. She'd brought so many problems into my life and held no remorse. She'd gotten her free pass to come and go as she pleased. This trial was just a formality to fully cash in on her newfound freedom. Didn't she understand I was just a kid and this was too much for me to handle? Didn't she realize that her lie would send my father to jail, possibly for the rest of his life? Didn't she see how Grandma Helen was using her to get revenge? If I knew all this, even at my young age, then why didn't she?

To soothe my anger and despair, I repeated the Serenity Prayer over and over. I must have spoken it over fifty times that morning. The more I said it the stronger I became. Each word that came out of my mouth gave me power. It was a strength I didn't know I had.

Uneasiness had my nerves getting the best of me and thus, I had to urinate as soon as we arrived at the courthouse. I asked Ms. Dillan if I could use the restroom. Not looking up from her paperwork, she pointed her ink pen towards the door and mumbled, "Make it quick, we don't have much time."

Barely able to hold it, I did the pee-pee dance back and forth, as I shimmied into a stall. I heard the restroom door open behind me but I was in such a rush that I didn't pay much attention. That is, until I smelled my mother's signature scent, Keri lotion and cigarettes.

"Mama is that you?" I whispered.

Inspecting the adjacent stalls to make sure we were alone, she remained silent. Frozen like an ice sculpture, I didn't move from the toilet seat. Signaling the coast was clear, Mama reached her hand underneath the stall and squeezed my foot. I knew this was her way of giving me a hug, so I reached and squeezed her foot back.

In a voice just louder than a whisper, she said, "Kira, I need you to be strong."

"But Mama I can't," I cried. "They want me to tell lies on you and daddy. I'm scared."

"I can't be in here long, but remember what I told you. Serenity and truth. God will be with you. He is your shepherd. He will give you strength. Speak the truth and the truth will set you free."

Mama's final foot squeeze was a sign that our time was up. I reached back under the stall and squeezed her foot back. She left the restroom first. Then, I counted to fifty before I left. Like we practiced, Andrea took the stand first. Feeling like I needed to summon a few angels, I looked up toward heaven and began to say the Serenity Prayer:

God grant me the serenity to accept the things that I cannot change, the courage to change the things I can.

Before I got to the last part, I noticed I'd stopped shaking. The fighter in me emerged again and this time I was ready for war. The door opened. "Kira, they're ready for you."

Taking the stand, I took my oath and swore to tell the truth, the whole truth and nothing but the truth. I'd seen this scenario many times on television but it amused me that they actually make people say those lines in a real court of law. With an orchestrated stroll, the Assistant District Attorney approached the stand to begin his line of questioning just like we'd rehearsed.

"Have you ever witnessed your parents do drugs?"

I took a deep gulp and glanced over at my mom and dad. Daddy looked helpless. My heart ached for him but I had to be truthful. "Yes."

Mama shifted in her seat. Daddy lowered his head.

The questioning continued. "What type of drugs did you see them do?"

"I've seen them smoke marijuana."

"Have you ever seen them do any other drugs?"

I knew this was only going to make things worse and I couldn't believe I had to be the one to betray them. Flashing back to Mama's words to tell the truth, I said "No."

My response stunned the Assistant DA. Confused, he said, "Speak up."

"I said no," my voice echoed through the microphone placed on the stand before me. "I haven't seen them do any other drugs."

Although I suspected my parents did cocaine, I'd never actually seen them do it. So, in essence, that was the truth.

Startled by my answer, he decided to go onto the next question. "Has your father ever touched you in a way that made you feel uncomfortable?"

"No."

The prosecutor's eyes blinked. He asked again, "Has your father ever touched you in a private place on your body?"

"NO!"

"Let me make sure I'm clear, you're saying that your father, the man sitting at that table," he yelled as he pointed toward Daddy, "has never touched you in a way that made you feel uncomfortable?"

I'd found my voice. It was time for me to open my mouth and fight back. They weren't going to force me to tell a lie. They weren't going to make me betray my daddy who I knew was an innocent man. So, I took the one opportunity I had to throw a punch. Instead of my fists, I used my mouth.

"So you're clear, I've told you, that adjudicator lady, Ms. Dillan, and Dr. Glen, MY FATHER HAS NEVER TOUCHED ME IN AN INAPPROPRIATE WAY! He doesn't even spank me. You and nobody else are going to make me say anything that's not true. ARE YOU CLEAR NOW?"

The courtroom erupted with noise and the judge banged his gavel to gain some kind of composure. As I stepped down, the prosecutor asked for a temporary recess. The lawyer was livid. I heard him telling someone in the next room that I made him look like a fool. Little did he know, I was only getting started. These people hadn't listened to me before but I was going to make sure they heard me from then on. I had nothing to lose. They'd taken everything away from me.

After a brief recess, the Assistant DA put me back on the stand and went back to his line of rehearsed questions. "Have you ever seen your dad touch your sister inappropriately?"

"No."

During our trial prep, they encouraged me to answer yes to all the questions even though I hadn't seen my daddy touch my sister inappropriately. Although far from perfect, Daddy loved us the best he knew how and there was no way I was going to go along with their scheme.

Realizing I was damaging the case, the prosecutor abruptly announced, "No further questions."

My testimony caused the prosecution team to scramble. Tired of being a victim of other people's selfish agendas, I wasn't going to shut my mouth. Ms. Dillan entered the witness holding room like a fire-breathing dragon stomping toward me. She had gotten so close that we were nose to nose. I could smell Juicy Fruit on her breath. Through almost locked jaws, she asked, "What the hell was that? This was supposed to be a slam dunk case resting on your corroborating testimony."

I didn't know what corroborating meant but it didn't matter. They had unleashed a warrior in me and I could attack at will. "Lady, you better get out of my face and you better do it right now. You and nobody else is going to get me to tell a lie on my daddy."

My mouth gave me power. It got people's attention. Made them stop and listen. As long as I had God and my mouth, I could fight back, so I continued to stand my ground. "In about five seconds, you're going to get out of my face, either by choice or by force."

The little ten-year-old girl in me was gone. I'd crossed over to adulthood. My mouth, my tone, and my conviction, made people think twice. Needless to say, she backed away. I smelled fear all over her. When she knew she was close enough to grab the knob, she ran out of the room.

My testimony put a huge dent in the prosecution's case, forcing them to offer Daddy a plea deal. He got six months. I'd saved his life. I'd fought the battle and won, but the war wasn't over. Now, who was going to fight for me?

The next day at school, I called Ms. Dillan from the front office phone. She wasn't available so I left a message and asked her to come to my school instead of calling me back at Ms. Benjamin's house. We needed to talk in person.

Days had gone by before she eventually paid a visit to my school. Finally, I told Ms. Dillan about Jason's attacks and my fear of the foster home. I thought for sure she'd get me out of there immediately. Listening intently, she gave me a solemnly hopeless look before saying, "I don't have anywhere else to put you."

For some reason, I wasn't shocked. I didn't expect her to rescue me. Just as the adults before her had failed, I was forced to rescue myself.

CHAPTER 10

Mama was pursuing regaining custody of me so I knew it wouldn't be long before I went back home. I just needed to get out of Ms. Benjamin's house before Andrea's birthday. Wondering if I'd make it out in time, I glanced down and noticed an envelope on the passenger side floor by my foot. Ms. Dillan was giving me a ride back to my foster home and it must have fallen out of her bag when she got in the car. Zooming in closer, I saw my last name written on the front of it. I had to know what was in that envelope, so when she turned her back, I quickly picked it up and placed it in my coat pocket. I was a little anxious hoping Ms. Dillan wouldn't realize it was missing before I could get out the car. When we finally pulled up, I didn't even let the engine stop before I jumped out. Waving a quick goodbye to

Ms. Dillan I darted into the house. I flew past everyone and went straight to my room, not even bothering to say hello.

The envelope had already been opened so I pulled the paper out. I almost passed out when I read what it said:

Child's mother has been asked to divorce father as a condition to be granted custody of child. Mother refuses to divorce father and therefore it is recommended she not receive custody. Child will remain in foster care.

As I read the last words, I burst into tears. All hope was lost. I couldn't understand how my mother would refuse to do anything that could get me back home. Didn't she realize what I was going through? I told her all about it each time we visited. Why wouldn't she just divorce my dad. Anything that they asked her to do, she should've been willing to do. I placed the letter back in the envelope and then placed the envelope in my Rainbow Brite suitcase. Not knowing what else to do, I got on my knees and prayed. Pouring all my pain out to God, I released my hurt and fear. Then, suddenly, I felt a shift inside of me. Instead of just venting all my problems, I made a request:

God, I need you to show me exactly what to do.

For some reason, I stopped my prayer right there. It was as if there was nothing else to be said. I went to sleep that night with a certain calm. My calm came from prayer. Every time I prayed, God sent an Answer.

CHAPTER 11

The next night, I pulled my journal out of my Rainbow Brite suitcase. The tattered notebook was one of the few things I had left of my former life. I guess my mother knew it would help me release all the emotions had bottled inside. I wrote in it almost every night. I also wrote letters to God. I wrote letters to Mama and Daddy, pretending that my life was normal and that I was at my old school. I wrote letters to all the people in my life who weren't listening to my words. Flipping the pages, I came across a letter I wrote to the prosecutor. As I read it, I was prompted to write another. Only this letter was addressed to the judge and I was asking him to help get me out of the foster home.

Then it hit me. Write a real letter to the custody judge and mail it to him. It was God speaking to me. You can't tell me otherwise. My heart skipped a few beats because there was a voice talking to me so loud and clear that it scared me. I froze in place for a few seconds and then I heard the voice say:

Mail it to the address on that envelope you found yesterday.

I didn't hesitate a second longer. I quickly went in my book bag, grabbed some notebook paper, and I began to write.

Dear Judge,

My name is Kira, and I need your help. I am 10 years old and in foster care. I was attacked a couple of nights ago by my foster brother and no one has done anything about it. I told my caseworker, Judy Dillan, and still nothing has been done. I'm scared. I want you to know that I haven't always been a foster child. I had a loving family and I lived in a nice house with a swingset in the backyard. I was taken from my home because my sister said my dad was molesting her and me. He never touched me and I never saw him do anything to her. I believed my mom was fighting to get me back home, but I found a letter from you stating you won't grant her custody of me because she refuses to divorce my dad and remove the "perpetrator" from her home. My sister turns 18 in 2 weeks so soon she'll be gone and I will be left here alone. I don't know what might happen next.

Please help me,

Kira

When I asked Mrs. Michaels to mail it for me, she didn't hesitate to jump into action. She even bought the stamp and envelope. I had fourteen days until Andrea's birthday and time flew by. One day, while walking home from school, I saw Ms. Dillan's blue Datsun parked in Ms. Benjamin's driveway. My heart quickened as I wondered why she was there. Moving like a turtle, I walked slowly down the driveway and opened the screen door. I had no idea what awaited me.

As soon as I pushed the main door open, Ms. Dillan yelled, "What did you do? Why did you write that letter?"

Terrified, I thought the letter was sent to her instead of the judge. I didn't know how to respond. I never considered that she'd possibly receive my little scribe. Then, as if to calm my nerves, she said the words that would change my fate forever, "Get in the car. The judge ordered me to bring you to him immediately."

Ms. Dillan was dying to know what I had written in the letter and badgered me about it throughout the whole ride. Peering out the window, refusing to answer her, I prayed for God to let the judge move me from my foster home. Upon our arrival, we were met by a young woman who introduced herself and invited me to come back to meet with the judge in his private chamber. Hundreds of important-looking books cascaded up and down the walls making me a bit apprehensive. Was I about to speak to a judge? Was I supposed to call him

Your Honor? My questions were answered when he walked in and introduced himself.

With a cup of coffee in his left hand, he extended his free one before speaking. “Hello, I’m Judge Blake. You must be Kira?”

“Yes, sir,” I paused. “I am.”

He waddled past me toward his chair. “So you wrote me a letter, huh?”

My stomach fluttered with nerves, but I made sure to answer. “Yes sir, I did.”

As he sat he asked, “How’d you get my address?”

His question broke my trance which was set on the monstrous law books perched on book cases around his office.

“It was on the outside of an envelope I found in my caseworker’s car.”

My answer must have intrigued him because he stopped mid sip and sat his cup of coffee on the desk.

“Well who mailed the letter for you?”

“A nice lady across the street from my foster home.”

I knew I had his full attention, so I was ready to spill the beans. This was my chance and boy did I take it. I opened my mouth and told him everything. I recounted all the sordid details including the most recent events that I had omitted from my letter. Listening intently, he rubbed his chin, allowing me to talk until I ran out of breath.

Once I took a moment to inhale, he said, "You're a remarkable little girl. I don't think I've ever met any little girl quite like you and I definitely haven't come across anyone who had the courage to write me a letter."

"You're my last hope," I said while wiping a single tear that managed to escape from my watery eyes.

I prepared myself for my latest let down. Surprisingly, his next statement caught me off guard. "I'm going to move you. Is there anyone we can call who'll let you come live with them temporarily until we get you a permanent place that's suitable and safe?"

"As a matter of fact there is," I answered. "Aunt Elsie."

God came right on time, three days early to be exact. My sister was turning eighteen and moving out. Luckily, I'd be out of there too. Although this was the most horrible chapter of my life, it was my first personal experience of the power of prayer and words. Fortunately, it wasn't my last.

Answered Prayers

When I was little, I prayed to get dolls for Christmas. Now, I was praying for a home. I wanted some place, any place, that was safe and secure. Before this experience, I never understood how to bring things to God. After which, I realized there's many ways. For me, conversations with God were the key, and my journal was the tool to sort out those conversations. I'd talk to God about my issue and he'd help me sort it out via my journals.

Matthew 6:6 - "But when you pray, go away by yourself, shut the door behind you, and pray to your Father in private. Then your father, who sees everything, will reward you..."

The TAPS Method

Watching how the results of daily prayer and journaling transformed my life from a child to a woman, I realized just like my morning cup of coffee, this too had to be an essential part of my everyday routine. After I divorced my first husband and started delving into my journaling more, there was a noticeable shift in my attitude and behavior. I was getting my swagger back and my confidence was skyrocketing. Mornings had a new meaning. The sun seemed to be shining brighter and joy was slowly etching its way into my life. I'd found a routine, but, my new life as a single mom with two jobs and a side hustle, kept me quite busy. Determined to stay connected with

God, I had to devise a plan to make sure I didn't miss my prayer and journal time.

As a result, I developed a method called **TAPS**. Each letter in the word stood for a part of the format and each had a dual use. It could be applied to both journaling or prayer. This acronym made it easy to remember my format so I didn't waste time on distractions or trying to figure out what to do next during my time with God.

T is for Talk. Approach God in a conversational manner. Don't immediately begin begging God to fix all your problems. Talk to him like you would a friend who you respect and admire, your mentor. You wouldn't start a conversation with your mentor by dropping bombs of problems on them, would you? In addition, show gratitude. **T**is also a reminder to be thankful. Thank God for everything, small and big.

A is for Ask. Request forgiveness and guidance. This is where I ask God to forgive me of my sins. In this moment, I don't try to hide anything because God already knows your thoughts and what you harbor in your heart. Forgiveness from God enables you to be forgiving to others. Also ask God for direction and guidance. You'll always make the right decision when you go to God first instead of handling things with foolish gut reaction.

P is for Pray. Prayer is like weightlifting. It's where spiritual muscle is built. Prayer changes things and that isn't just a cliché. Remember, prayer isn't one sided. Yes, prayer is for talking to God about your problems and asking for guidance but one of the biggest lessons I learned as a child is to take a moment and be quiet. If you shut your mouth during prayer, you can hear God speak back and guide you.

S is for Scripture. You must know the word to live the word. I don't mean memorizing it verbatim. I couldn't begin to tell you the chapter names and verses of the many scriptures I use throughout my day. However, I know they exist because I've taken time to read, write, and speak them. Memorizing God's word might make you seem more credible in the eyes of religious folk, but that's not my focus. My only purpose is to know scripture to help me fight my battles.

This method was so effective that I ended up eliminating mind wandering distractions before they could pop up and essentially waste precious time that could've been spent communicating with God. Also, I found that I could use it whether I had as little as five minutes or if I had hours. Essentially, **The TAPS Method** enabled me to witness my prayer and journal life mature which allowed me to tackle even bigger issues, like forgiveness, motherhood, love, joy, and peace. Prayer and journaling helped me envision the steps God wanted me to take.

CHAPTER 12

I'd landed inside a fairy tale at Aunt Elsie's house. Floor-scrubbing Cinderella had disappeared and become a princess overnight. Waltzing into a fully decorated room with ruffled white curtains, a plush comforter set, throw pillows, and a fluffy rug, made me feel like I was in a fairytale. Top that with the fact that I didn't have to share it with anyone, I was literally in heaven on Earth. Floor to ceiling shoes covered one wall of the room. Multi-colored church dresses and five different winter coats filled my closet. To me, this was unbelievable because at home with my parents I was lucky to get a Members Only jacket. Custom sewn Easter suits had become my norm along with drawers full of outfits for every occasion. I had the latest fashion from leather coats to riding boots. I'd even begun to have an impressive disc collection with a Walkman CD player and headphones. If you didn't know me, you'd assume I was a spoiled only child. But it was all a charade. I was still a foster girl who traded the evil foster mother for Mommy Dearest herself.

Aunt Elsie might as well had been a politician whose only concern was keeping up appearances. I played the role of her public representative so she kept me on point and dressed to the tee. Quite good at faking it, I played the role of the beautiful happy princess. In reality, I was petrified that if I wasn't perfect, I'd go back to the foster home or be put out on the streets. To show my gratitude, Aunt Elsie demanded that I keep her house spotless and always praise her in public for taking me in.

Somewhat of a celebrity at her church, my aunt made it clear that we were to be flawless for every service. Knowing I had to have all my chores done before I'd be allowed to go anywhere on Saturdays, I'd usually wash my hair the night before. One time, I was in a bit of a rush and accidently left a few strands of hair in the kitchen sink. Being a stickler for keeping her home spotless, Aunt Elsie noticed it immediately. Just as I'd finished pulling my hair into a high ponytail to sit down under the dryer, she stormed in with her eyes squinted like an angry bull.

Before I could ask her what was wrong, she said, "You don't think enough of my house to clean your hair out of the sink, huh?"

Unsure of what the right answer was, I replied, "Oh, I'm sorry, I'll go clean it."

But, it was too late. Before I could blink, she had scissors in her hand and cut my entire ponytail clean off the top of my head. Beautiful bushels of hair, which normally hung to the middle of my back, tumbled into my lap. Stunned, I patted the top of my head. All my tresses were gone.

"You're going to appreciate all I do for you," she hissed, "or just like your hair, you'll be gone too."

To top it all off, she took me to the hair salon the next day and forced me to get a Jheri curl.

Constantly, she reminded me that I was her little charity case. She'd repeat the following as if it were a chorus to her favorite song:

I know you're not used to anything, but you're going to take care of my stuff.

Clean up after yourself. You should be glad I don't put you of my house.

If I did everything perfect, life was manageable. I wasn't unhappy but I wasn't particularly joyful either. It was like living in gray. There's nothing wrong with a colorless existence per se, except that it lacks feeling, life, and energy. You're just there, blending in.

When I arrived, everything I owned could fit in my tiny Rainbow Brite suitcase. Aunt Elsie made sure to remind me of this as often as she could. Dealing with her daily judgment and criticism, I showed my appreciation for her adopting me by doing everything I could do to make her happy. However, my eagerness to please her created a fake version of myself and forced me to live on eggshells. The real me was insecure and I hated who I was forced to become. Kira wasn't good enough so I lived in a world where I pretended to see rainbows despite the heavy rain clouds above my head. Gloomy and gray was my every day forecast. Nevertheless, if I wanted to stay in Aunt Elsie's world, I had to pretend.

I'd be the first to volunteer for leadership roles at church in the youth ministry. This would give her plenty to brag about. She'd love to hear her church friends say what a fine job she was doing raising that poor child and how much of a saint she was to take me in. Many days, I had wished I could skip church and disappear instead of faking like I was happy being her charity case.

The only bright spot was my sister-cousin, Vicki. Being that she was much older, she'd stop by almost every day to to chat and hang out. On Saturdays, we'd cruise down Candler Road blasting music in her Mustang 5.0 and have the time of our lives. It was such a contrast to being stuck home with the constant gloom and doom I faced each day. With Vicki, I had sunshine and energy. Everybody was out. Washing cars, grilling, or just making the most of the day. She was my ray of light but as soon as she left, everything would go back to gray.

Still, I found the silver-lining. Life with Aunt Elsie exposed me to much more than what my mother and father could have ever given me. When living at home, I'd never traveled further than Macon, Georgia, where Big Mama lived. So when Aunt Elsie announced we were taking a vacation, I nearly leapt out of my skin. Naive and underexposed I thought vacations were only for rich people. I was ecstatic and looked forward to it like a kid on Christmas. Of course, Aunt Elsie had to get glory for exposing me to something new. As I eavesdropped on her nightly church gossip sessions, I listened to her tell church member after church member how she took me to Rich's Department Store to buy me my first piece of luggage.

"Ain't no way she's traveling with me with that ratty little bag she likes to carry. I took her to the mall and got her some good luggage," she'd say.

Part of me was thrilled about going away but the other part of me wanted to tell her to take her luggage and shove it. Too fearful of going back to the shelter though, I'd just shut my mouth.

Criticism washer method of refining me and keeping my stature on point. She never wanted me to get too relaxed and forget my manners. Dinner was tense as I obsessed over which fork to use. If I even thought about putting my elbow on the table for one second, she'd remind me that I ate dinner like a poor child who couldn't be taken anywhere.

Forced to read etiquette books, I became an expert in proper demeanor. Regardless of how I was treated, she gave me a few life lessons that would later serve me well especially when my money was low.

Additionally, and maybe this sounds shallow, she taught me how to shop. Her idea of shopping wasn't just about spending money or getting a retail adrenaline rush. Shopping had to have a purpose. Because of her, I developed a keen eye for quality clothes that could transition well into different occasions. I'd become a young expert at selecting garments that would last for years and survive fashion trends. Making ten dollars look like a hundred was my specialty and I could find creative ways to wear my clothes by mixing high end pieces with low end knock offs.

A model in her younger days, Aunt Elsie knew everything about beauty. Healthy eating and weight management were important to her before it became an Instagram hashtag trend. She taught me how to polish my nails, exfoliate my feet and to never buy cheap shoes. Before I was eighteen, I'd learned at least a hundred uses for Vaseline like applying it to wet skin immediately out the shower to keep your body feeling soft and gentle like a baby's bottom. Mixing the oily supplement with perfume made the fragrance last longer and dabbing it on your earlobes would allow your earrings to easily slide through the pierced holes. All these tips were for show but they have stood the test of time and I still use them to this day.

Unfortunately, that's where Aunt Elsie's concern stopped. If she couldn't get recognition or praise, she had no interest. My school achievements meant nothing to her – not even my placement on the Honor Roll. See, there were no church members there to give her the praise she craved so she simply ignored it as if my intelligence didn't even matter.

Still, I worked extremely hard in school and always made straight A's which earned me a coveted spot on the Principal's List. Every semester I'd invite Aunt Elsie to my Awards Ceremony and secretly hoped she'd maybe one day show up. Sadly, on Awards Day, I'd search the crowd to find not one familiar face there supporting me. Not Mama, not Daddy, and not Aunt Elsie. Other kids got raging applause from their family members when their names were called while I'd be fighting back tears as the teachers managed a few polite claps to cheer me on. I knew they only did it out of pity. Still, I pushed through and got accepted to several colleges.

Things seemed to be turning around when I received a scholarship to my dream school, Spelman College. I should've known that joy would be short lived since Aunt Elsie forbade me to go to a Black school. Because it was an HBCU, it wouldn't have given her the bragging rights she craved, especially since I'd also earned an academic scholarship to the

University of Georgia. Being all about appearances, the lush green grass, manicured bushes, and beautiful campus wooed her. Attending UGA symbolized the good job she did in raising me. Continuing my front, I was once again in a place where I had no voice and no control over my happiness. I faked excitement knowing deep down that prissy school, with its lilly white students, just wasn't for me.

After my high school graduation, my goal of going off to college had become a reality. Little did I know how quickly the dream would be shattered. Aunt Elsie drove me to the campus in Athens, Georgia and as we pulled into the dorm parking lot, she drove past all the parking spaces.

Curious, I asked, "Why are you passing all the parking spaces?"

"Oh, I'm making a U-turn."

"A U-turn?" My eyebrows raised in confusion. "Can't you just pull into that spot right there?"

"I'm not staying," she laughed as if my question was amusing. "I gave you a roof over your head and made sure you went off to college. My job is done. You're grown now. You gotta figure it out."

Her words were detached as if she was talking to a stranger instead of someone who had lived in her home for the last eight years. Instantly, the little bit of security I felt had dropped from underneath me. I was ten-years-old again. Helpless. Speechless. Angry. Powerless.

With her engine still running, she waited long enough for me to get my things from the car. I closed the trunk and walked toward her door, expecting at least a hug. Emotionless, she waved goodbye and drove off. There I was, left on the curb like an old piece of furniture being dumped in a back alley. She didn't walk in to see my dorm room, didn't offer a hand in bringing my things upstairs, and didn't bother to help me get settled. She didn't even leave me any money. But what did I expect? Wasn't that the job of Mama and Daddy? Aunt Elsie was just glad to have me out of her hair and gone from her house.

Hurt and anger brewed inside of me. I thought of Andrea and Grandma Helen. They had robbed me of the opportunity to feel how proud Mama and Daddy would be seeing me go off to college. Robbed me of love and support. Robbed me of security. Robbed me of a home.

Although I didn't want to admit it, I really was nothing more than an unwanted, unloved foster child – even still. Maybe Ms. Benjamin was right after all.

Aunt Elsie

Living with her wasn't my fondest memory but she taught me some valuable lessons that would stay with me forever. These teachings shaped the woman I'd become. I didn't realize it then but Aunt Elsie was trying to show me how to be a lady. She wanted to make sure that I could handle business and be able to put my emotions to the side so they didn't cloud my judgment. Even though her methods weren't the most practical, and despite her lack of motherly love, she made me a boss – even before I knew what that word really meant. She'd planted the seeds that would sprout later in life. She taught me to be self-sufficient, smart with my money, see the value in traveling and the importance of an education. No matter what happened in life, nobody could ever strip me of the values she instilled. She was showing me how to be a ***Glow Getter***. Although her methods were unconventional, she had a lot of wisdom. I'm forever thankful she planted those seeds in me because she was teaching me how to be a Proverbs 31 Woman.

Proverbs 31:25 "She is clothed with strength and dignity, and she laughs without fear of the future..."

While journaling this experience, I was led to make what I called my ***Glow Getter*** list. It contains goals, dreams, and directions that I feel God is giving me so that I can execute those items on my list. Doubling my income was the first thing I wanted to accomplish. When I first started my corporate career, I worked two jobs and sold Avon on the side. However, I knew I couldn't do that forever. I'd been researching schools to further my education and had found the program in which I wanted to enroll. As I journaled about this one night while sipping tea, I looked up and gazed at my mug. The saying on the mug was, **Face Your Fears**.

When I purchased the mug, I wanted it to give me the courage to put my pieces back together. Yet, as the message jumped out at me, I knew it was meant for so much more. Knowing this wasn't just a coincidence, I took immediate action. Early that next morning, I went online and filled out an enrollment application. My admission decision came within days. It was official, I was going back to school.

This was a giant leap of faith toward increasing my income. It was time to move past fear and level up. Managing money was next on my list. With two mouths to feed, no one to lean on, and no safety net, money management was a must. I studied Dave Ramsey's financial principles, created a budget, and stuck tightly to it. Meal planning and couponing became daily hobbies. A standard would be set in my household and it was up to me to model it. I'd made stupid mistakes while searching for what I thought I was missing but God showed me it wasn't too late to correct those blunders.

Determined to be the best version of me and destined to not let all I'd been through be in vain, I wrote the following mission statement in my journal:

I am committed to living my life in such a way that I am an inspiration to my sons and others. I place a strong emphasis on caring for myself emotionally, spiritually, and physically. I wish to be an example of how to lead a fulfilling life by not allowing life's circumstances and situations to determine my destiny. I stay reminded that only I can control my happiness and satisfaction with life. I set goals and strive until I achieve them. I am committed to bridging my energy, enthusiasm, and gregarious personality with my love of reading, writing, computer skills, and administrative talent in order to have a fulfilling personal and professional life. I am committed to devoting the time necessary to develop my skills and gain experience. I am committed to enjoying the process even when it gets hard. I am committed to raising my sons to become God-fearing, self-aware, confident, poised, and educated men. I am committed to spending time with God. I am committed to consciously invest in myself, and I am committed to three promises: I promise to protect my spiritual, emotional, and physical health. I promise to forgive myself when I fall short or stumble on this journey. And I promise to not apologize to anyone for being me.

Signed,

Kira

With unshakeable resolve plus my mission statement, I'd masterfully play the cards I was dealt. I'd prove that my circumstances wouldn't dictate my outcomes. Although I was an unwanted foster child, God showed me I didn't have to stay that way. Embarrassment motivated me to strike back with my mouth when I felt ashamed. It was time to overcome this obstacle. Putting my disgrace to the side, I rolled up my sleeves, pulled out the books, and handled business. With God's perfect timing you can go from the basement to the penthouse suite. All you must do is get aligned with God and your soul. Then, you Glow GET it!

CHAPTER 13

Carrying my belongings down the dormitory hallway, I held back hot tears each time I passed another student who had family members by their side. Passing by a room where a mother helped her daughter make the bed, I paused for a moment and watched them from the hallway. I'd wished my life was different. There was no logical reason for me to have been the one taken away from my home. Why had God allowed me to be robbed of the love that I needed? I was broken and worthless. I was alone and invisible. I was fighting a private battle. It was me against my anger.

College life was rough with no emotional support and very little money. When everyone went home for weekends and holidays, I stayed at the dorm. Aunt Elsie had essentially washed her hands of me and made it clear that she didn't want me running back to her house. Also, I no longer had any type of relationship with Mama or Daddy. Depression set in after she lost custody of me, so she'd withdrawn from the world and completely cut ties from everyone including Grandma Helen and Andrea. Longing for the love and guidance of a mother, I'd call her occasionally, but the conversations were dry. Our mother-daughter bond was lost.

Lacking my mother's guidance, I'd grown bitter and insecure. My identity was lost and I desperately yearned for security. I'd entered a never-ending search to find me. Dealing with so much inner turmoil, coupled with having no support, financially or emotionally, I withdrew from college and moved back to the city. It would be the first of many mistakes to come.

Needing a place to stay in Atlanta, I called my godmother Fran. She and Mama were best friends in high school and from the day I was born, she thought of me as her daughter. She'd gone through her own personal struggles but kept in close contact. Finally, back on her feet, she welcomed me into her tiny apartment with open arms.

Although she lived in a one-bedroom with two children of her own, she made space for me. The maternal love she showed me helped to fill part of my void but still, I longed for the relationship that I'd lost with my birth mom. Nevertheless, God's ***grace*** is always sufficient and Fran was the praying mother that God saw fit for me. She wanted me to realize that I wasn't alone and assured me that although she didn't have lots of money, she had plenty of time. She was there when I needed her most.

Her dedication gave me hope but didn't fully erase my need to feel stable. No matter what I did, gray clouds still followed me. It felt like I'd been living in a rain shower where the sun refused to come out. I just wanted to live in sunshine for a change. Was that too much to ask?

Talking to Fran about this one day, she said something that I'd forever hold dear:

The sun always shines after the rain. Talk to God. That's all you have to do.

She didn't know it but she sparked hope inside of me. I was so lost in my bitterness that I'd stopped praying. Stopped speaking to God. Stopped journaling. All the tools that I had once used to change my life, I'd abandoned. It was time to get back on track. It was time to heal myself. So, that night, I prayed. I opened my Bible. I wrote my thoughts, words, and feelings in my journal. After a while, things seemed like they were beginning to look up for me. Still living with a deep regret of dropping out of college, I prayed to God for a sign.

One day, unexpectedly, Aunt Elsie called me.

"That nice boy Evan came by here looking for you. He left his number. Call him."

Now, Aunt Elsie doesn't go out of her way to do things like that so I took it as a sign from God.

Evan was a guy that I had met at Moseley Park during my senior year of high school. Back then, parks on Sundays were just as popular as night clubs. You never knew who you might meet. Guys pulled out their freshly washed whips just to cruise the park. Girls strolled around to showcase their booty shorts and catch the eye of a baller. Our outfits were revealing way too much skin but that was the point, right?

We pulled up to the park and got out the car to show off. I had on some Daisy Dukes with my name airbrushed on the back and fringes on the bottom that showed just a peek of booty cheek. I was prancing all around showing off my thick thighs. You couldn't tell me nothing. Car hopping, we could pick and choose which guys we'd give the time of day. I loved being seen but quickly tired of talking, so I began dismissing several guys and limiting my conversation. Ready to walk further into the park, I waited for my friends to finish their conversations. While waiting, impatiently might I add, an Al B. Sure look-alike approached me and laid his game down super slick.

"Can I get my turn now?" he asked.

He wasn't my type at all but I didn't want to appear stuck up or rude. Besides arrogance was an easy way to get cussed out and embarrassed in front of everybody in the park. Seeing he had my attention, he jumped out of his black Acura Legend, to introduce himself.

"I'm Evan, what's your name?"

"Kira." My response was curt because I wasn't the least bit interested but I continued with the conversation if only to pass the time.

"You from Atlanta?"

"Yes." After peeping out his shiny car, I said, "I see you have a Florida State tag. You from there?"

"I'm from Atlanta, but I live in Tallahassee," he explained. "I'm a student at Florida State University."

Now that got my attention. He was a college student. Aunt Elsie's voice echoed in the back of my head:

Get you a man that's got something going for himself. One who is going to have a good job and some benefits.

Instantly impressed, I gave him my number.

I had him pick me up from Aunt Elsie's house for our first date. As soon as I introduced her to Evan, I could tell she was impressed by his polite manners and the fact that he attended Florida State. He fit perfectly into the fairy tale she liked to present to everyone. Aunt Elsie asked about his family and when he mentioned that both his parents were college graduates, she became his biggest groupie – oh, I mean, his biggest fan.

From that point forward, each time we went on a date, she nearly pushed me out the door while giving me the '*he's a keeper*' thumbs up signal behind his back. I should've known not to take her advice on men because her marriage was a sham. There was no love. Her husband made a very good living so she was only there for money and security. It was very clear that she didn't like her husband. They had an arrangement. He worked and paid all the bills while she stayed pretty and spent his money.

My first red flag occurred on our first date when he bragged about himself the entire time. I should have run for the hills right then. Come to think of it, he didn't hold any doors open for me and he made it a point to check himself out in every mirror we passed. He even had the nerve to tell me I could end up with the coveted spot of his girlfriend if I play my cards right. Foolishly I excused his arrogance and narcissism because, as Aunt Elsie said, he was going places.

We hung out a few more times over the summer, but every time we got together, his conceit grated my last nerve. When I left for college, we ended up losing contact. So for him to stop by Aunt Elsie's to get in touch with me, came as a total surprise. Maybe this was my chance to have a better life. Taking Aunt Elsie's advice, I called him. We chatted and played catch up. He told me he would be graduating in a year. As a college dropout, I really admired his tenacity. Aunt Elsie's words echoed in my mind again. I guess he really was going places. Maybe she was onto something.

Sparks with Evan were nonexistent and the more I was around him the more I realized not only was he arrogant and narcissistic but he was also selfish, judgmental, and critical. Having the wrong guidance on how to choose a man coupled with my desperation for security and stability, I concluded he was a good guy because he was going somewhere in life. Evan met all the characteristics per Aunt Elsie's checklist. Therefore, I ignored my God-given intuition and said yes when, after a few years of dating, he asked me to marry him.

Right in line with Aunt Elsie's prediction, Evan graduated college and found a good job. I found out I was expecting before we got married, so we moved in together and pushed up the wedding date. I didn't feel great about the decision but I'd finally have the security and stability that I'd been searching for throughout my childhood. Deep down though, I knew he wasn't the one.

Subjected to daily criticism and snide remarks, I'd become a ticking time bomb. Whenever we had a disagreement, he'd throw up my relationship with my mother. He even stooped so low as to share this information with his own mom, my soon to be monster-in-law. Even though every fiber in me said not to go along with the marriage, I put my need for security and stability before using my good sense. The night before I married Evan, I received a very clear omen that he wasn't the one.

My relationship with his mother was awful. Her temperament toward me reminded me of how Grandma Helen treated my father. She was just as evil and conniving. Always stirring up trouble, and not just for us, but with everyone she encountered. Whenever she was in the building, drama was always nearby. Never approving of me, she made it a point to criticize how I kept house or undermine me with my son. The strife between us was so thick you could cut it with a knife. Although I was supposed to be the blushing bride, I wasn't afforded the opportunity to make any of the wedding plans. Evan's ego wouldn't allow it. He and his mother did all the planning since they were the ones with all the money. My only role was to be a pretty face in a white gown.

His mother stopped by our house the day before the wedding. I'd gone out earlier for my final dress fitting and they didn't hear me come in. Approaching the kitchen, I could overhear their conversation. His mother was doing what she does best, stirring up mess.

"I don't even understand why you're marrying her. She doesn't have any class. No education and nothing to bring to the table. Shoot, she wasn't even raised by her mother."

Her words cut deep and, unfortunately, they were somewhat true. Even though I was saddened, I wasn't going to stand there and let her get away with saying them. My blood was boiling with anger as I stepped into the kitchen with a few choice words of my own.

"No class, huh?" I yelled, as I placed my hands upon my hip and twisted my neck, like a snake, with every syllable. "You forgot that I know the real you. I know where you come from. Your fake front doesn't fool me."

Stunned that I'd overheard their conversation, she tried her best at damage control.

"I was only suggesting that you go back to college, love. I'm sorry you don't have your mother to tell you these things."

The way she used the word love, set me off. It was condescending and lacked substance. I had initially tried my best to hold back this tongue lashing she so rightfully deserved but after she brought up my mother, I'd lost it.

"You weren't always a college graduate. You didn't come from money like you want to pretend you did. You forgot that you grew up with nothing more than a whorish alcoholic mother who had five children by five different men. You don't even know who your daddy is. At least, I know mine. So take a long look in the mirror before you talk about someone else's family."

Evan stood silent like a scared little boy. There was no heart in him anyway so he didn't bother to diffuse the situation. In retrospect, I shouldn't have been so rude to his mother. After all, she was my elder and deserved some level of respect. But, the words had already left my lips and couldn't be retracted.

Evan

Don't marry him. That's all I kept telling myself on our wedding day. However, we had a child, had been together a few years, and I didn't have anywhere else to go. Plus, I wanted a stable family for my son. All justifiable reasons, right? But fear is what really egged me on.

Sensing my hesitancy to go through with it, Fran asked, "Are you sure you want to marry him?"

She didn't know Evan very well but the few times she'd met him, his arrogance offended her. Also, she knew his mother had tainted my relationship with the rest of the family through her gossip and disrespectful comments. Fran knew I was marrying into problems.

I saw all the warning signs; I just didn't stop. During wedding photos, I didn't smile. I knew he wasn't the one God had sent me. He wouldn't even look me in my eyes as we stood at the altar. Fighting the urge to be a runaway bride, I kept telling myself this would make my life better. But saying 'I do' didn't change a thing. In fact, it only made one thing worse – my mouth!

Having no genuine Godly guidance on what to look for in a man, I settled for the gray life that came with being with Evan. Privately, I was suffering. I wanted sunshine. I felt like I was back with my Aunt Elsie and living each day to avoid criticism. Daily, I suffered as he made it his job to belittle me by constantly throwing up my dysfunctional family and making fun of my nonexistent relationship with my mother. Narcissism made him throw jabs at my upbringing so he could feel better. After a while, it was clear to me why Aunt Elsie adored him. They shared the same character flaws. He too was only concerned about his appearance. Conceit was his claim to fame. He even had the audacity to believe he was better because he held a college degree. Just like Aunt Elsie, he treated me as if he'd done me a favor by taking me in. Evan was all the right things on paper but that's as far as it went. Young and naive, I didn't realize the important role prayer played in relationships.

Psalms 139:14 "I will praise you for I am fearfully and wonderfully made. Marvelous are your works, and that my soul knows very well..."

God was on a roll in my life but there was still work he wanted me to do on me. With so much going on, I began to designate a day of the week to journal on a specific area of my life. Cruel treatment, judgment, and criticism had long lasting effects. Honestly, I didn't know my self-worth and always questioned if I was good enough whenever I was around women outside my immediate circle. No matter the setting, whether it was baby showers, dinners, birthdays, I always noticed a pattern. I either encountered women who immediately liked me and seemed to be drawn to me enough where we could have instant conversation and eventual friendships **OR** I'd encounter women who displayed hate, jealousy, and disdain for me. I felt the need to make sure that these women, the haters, knew how I felt. They'd throw an underhanded insult and I'd quickly jab right back. I couldn't take the high road.

The therapy that I received through journaling was enlightening. I realized, it wasn't about them and how they felt about me. They were merely projecting towards me their personal insecurities. I'd join right in and do the same. Then, there'd be a tennis match of lobs and insults. I'd later realize, through journaling, that their opinions of me weren't as important as my opinion about myself. As soon as I stopped allowing my own insecurities to push me toward proving I was enough, worthy to be accepted and liked, I didn't feel the need to go back and forth arguing with them. God had allowed shameful events in my life so that I could be perfectly imperfect. My childhood gave me a story and a resilient soul. Once, I could love and accept myself for being fearfully and wonderfully made, joy flooded into my life. I was created by the most high God and I had come to a point where I didn't have to defend myself. I was still perfect in God's eyes and the proof was right in the Bible. I didn't need Evan, his mother, or any group of high siddity women to tell me otherwise.

CHAPTER 14

Married life made my mouth spiral out of control. Evan didn't deserve my respect and I surely didn't give it to him. In every discussion, I found myself quick to retaliate with my words. I couldn't allow things to be left unchecked. My issues then started spilling beyond my household. If someone had a problem with me, I would walk right up to them and ask them point blank, "Do you have an issue that you want to get off your chest?"

No matter where I went, I was getting into arguments with other people. If the grocery store clerk made a smart comment, I'd make one right back. If the drive through person made a mistake with my order, I'd blow a gasket just to let them know they screwed up. If I said hello and someone didn't speak back, I'd have something to say about that too. What was wrong with me? Why was I so edgy and fight ready? I couldn't help but wonder, why couldn't I shut my mouth?

God was trying to tell me something but I wasn't listening. Eventually, he used my son to get my attention. A group of friends and I took our kids to Applebee's for dinner. I was sensing an attitude from our waitress. Out of all the people at the table, she chose to show her nasty and rude side to me. She said one thing out of line and it had pushed me over the edge. With the left corner of my top lip raised and a red laser beam stare, I was ready to go off. Before I could check her, I heard my son say to another kid, "Oh no, she pulled the pin."

Turning in his direction to make sure I heard him clearly, I asked, "What did you say?"

"Mom, you're like a grenade waiting to go off. Anytime someone does something to you, you explode on them," he said before going back to chomping on his half-eaten burger.

I was aware that I had an issue with my mouth but I never stopped to think that my kids were aware of it too. It was time to take an assessment. I was carrying emotional scars along, and the wounds that Evan had given me on a daily basis had only made them bleed. Was this what marriage was supposed to be like? I'd married a man with no character. Someone lacking the consideration a husband should have for a wife. I'd married someone who wouldn't defend me against his mother's attacks or attempt to bring peace to the situation. I'd married someone who didn't care if I made it home safely. I'd promised forever to a man who didn't bother opening doors for me. I'd given my all to someone who used his money to control me. Worst of all, I'd married someone who didn't pray. Once I realized we weren't equally yoked, I decided it was time for me to do some work. Some work on me, and some work on my marriage.

Prayer became a part of my daily routine, but if things were going to get better with Evan, we needed to pray together. Figuring reading the Bible was the first place to start, I asked him to read some scriptures with me. He laughed. The Bible was a joke to him. Still believing he was smarter than everyone else, he debated every scripture. Accepting my mistake, I acknowledged it was hopeless. I'd married the wrong man.

Still, I kept praying and writing in my journal. I didn't want to be a divorce statistic. My sons deserved to be raised in a two-parent household but how could I continue in this uncomfortable charade? Avoiding the verbal abuse and constant arguing led Evan and I to live separate lives. I was a single woman with a marriage certificate. When Evan was home, he'd hang out downstairs playing video games, while I was upstairs taking care of our sons, reading, or writing in my journals. How could this be the life that God intended for me?

After a while, my instincts were signaling that something was different with Evan. One night, a voice in my head told me to get up and go downstairs. It was late, about one thirty in the morning. I tiptoed down the stairs leading from our master suite. Once I realized he was sleeping on the couch, I slid his cell phone toward me with my foot. Picking it up in one fell swoop, I rushed back to the stairs to search through it. What I found shocked me. There were naked pictures of different women on his phone but several from one girl in particular. When I checked his call history, he had call after call from the same number. Apparently they talked numerous times throughout the day. The trail of text messages was long enough to write a book. I wasn't surprised or upset. It all made sense. Placing the phone back in its original spot, I went back to bed. Once again, I had to plan an escape route.

For the next three months, my nightly phone checks revealed him to be in a full-blown relationship with the naked picture girl. Finally, I confronted him. Lies and denial dripped from his tongue like a faucet. Weak, I'd accepted the verbal abuse. Broken, I'd accepted his emotional abuse. But no way was I going to accept cheating. I deserved better. I was nobody's victim.

The next Monday, I filed for divorce. Petrified, I spoke to the lawyer. He explained we'd have to go to court to settle things and how it could get ugly. My childhood court experience came to mind. But I was a fighter with two sons who were looking up to me. They weren't going to watch their mother be a victim. They would grow up knowing how to be a real man and how to treat their wives.

The day the divorce papers were served, we were both still living in the house we bought together. Arrogance wouldn't allow Evan to accept that I had the audacity to divorce him so he was infuriated when the sheriff knocked on the door.

Evan's twisted nose and squinted eyes made me fully aware that his ego had received a death blow. Therefore, I wasn't surprised when he tried to play on my insecurities.

Within minutes of receiving the papers, he was on verbal attack mode. "Who do you think is going to want you? You have two kids, no education, and no money. I did you a favor by marrying you. I promise you, no one else is going to want you."

Nonchalantly, I ignored him and started folding clothes. My lack of attention didn't stop his barrage of insults.

Tired of it, I fired back and when I did, I unloaded. "You think I care about you throwing a tantrum like a little bitch?"

Boy, those words must have been a trigger because he pushed me into the linen closet. As he stood over me, he screamed, "You got a lot of mouth. What you need is someone to bust you in it."

What he didn't know was those were fighting words to me. I pushed him off of me with the strength of a thousand wrestlers. I planned on sending him out of there by one of two ways, a stretcher or a hearse.

Once again, God wanted to get my attention, so he used my son who cried out, "Mama please don't kill Daddy."

I didn't realize it but I had a pair of scissors in my hand that I'd grabbed off the dresser. Backed into a corner, the only place for Evan to go was out the window. Distracted by my son's voice, Evan used that second to charge at me. I swung the scissors like a Chinese star hoping to hit him in the throat. I missed only by inches. We'd both gone too far. Evan quickly headed down the steps and out the door. He didn't come home until late that night. Crisis averted but I knew I wouldn't be able to shut my mouth until the next incident.

Realizing two people divorcing can't live under the same roof, I asked him to pack some belongings and move. Controlled by ego and narcissism, Evan refused. He said I should be the one to leave since I was filing the divorce. And that's just what I did.

The Wrong Man

Because of my upbringing, I didn't know what to look for in marriage. I needed a man who was strong enough to lead and love. My mouth wasn't the problem with Evan. He just wasn't the man to whom God wanted me to submit.

Ephesians 5:22 - "Wives submit to your own husbands, as to the Lord..."

My mind viewed submission as a sign of weakness and my only defense to weakness had always been my mouth. Sometimes, I didn't say enough and sometimes I said too much. I could see my mouth rear its ugly head a time or two in my relationship with Mark, my second husband. Even though he was patient with me, I needed to get a handle on it ASAP.

For years, I'd associated submission to passivity but I discovered this isn't true. Submission meant that I was strong enough to have control over my mouth and wise enough to be aware of my words. Therefore, when I submitted to my husband, I was actually submitting to God. Submission isn't about whether or not the man deserves it. It's about following God's design. Submitting pleases God.

There will come a time when I'll need to allow my husband to lead and perhaps make a mistake or two. However, I know we'll still be blessed as long as I submit and respect his leadership. Husbands were meant to lead their homes and whenever there is corruption to this design, problems occur. My father didn't lead our home. He followed my mother who was being led by her own mother, and I was an eyewitness to the problems that resulted from that. My childhood trauma was enough of an example to shut my mouth and follow God's design.

CHAPTER 15

Tons of hopes, dreams, wishes, and plans had been bottled up inside of me. I had no idea how or where to begin to achieve them but I had faith the size of a mustard seed. Just one foot in front of the other. Going against the grain was my norm. Time after time, God had shown me all I had to do was take the first step and he'd do the rest.

Enjoying coffee on the small balcony of my apartment, I wondered why God had me leave my home and move into an apartment. I'd been obedient to God, and although I was content, I wanted another home. Apartment living was quite different from living in a house. My sons were young and all over the place. Our small abode limited their activities. Constantly, I had to remind them not to jump or make noise that would disrupt our neighbors. They didn't have a yard to play ball in or run around like children should.

Like always, I journaled about it and started doing a bit of research. From the looks of things, being that my name was still on the house I shared with Evan, my debt-to-income ratio couldn't support the purchase of another home. Discussing this with my attorney, his advice was to file bankruptcy since the real estate market had crashed and everyone was upside down in their homes anyway. But God saw differently. Because I was obedient, God blessed me with another home exactly twelve months from the date I moved out of my house. I closed on my home only days before my lease was up. His perfect timing struck again.

God didn't bless me with just any home, he blessed me with the same exact home as the one I shared with Evan but for less than half the price. That's the favor of God. That's his ***grace***. The closer I got to God, the more I could recognize him in my life.

Even though I wasn't fully divorced, I truly believed God would one day send me the man he had for me. Receiving word that my divorce was final was like music to my ears calling for a celebration because that chapter was finally closed. God brought me through yet another storm. Pulling out my champagne glass and my journal, I had to write about this moment. But instead of writing about how great I felt to finally be divorced, my journal therapy led to the ***aha*** moment. I knew nothing about being a wife. I couldn't think of one example of healthy relationships or happy long-lasting marriages.

Soul Searching

Standing in my new surroundings, with all the empty space, devoid of the most basic household items like a can opener or even a chair, leftover remnants of the unwanted foster girl began to rise inside of me. Was this an inescapable fate? Once again I was starting over from ground zero. Lord what do I do now? Then it hit me. This was my chance to re-write my story. Tears began to fall, but not tears for starting over or tears from a failed marriage. My tears were cleansing me. God reminded me this wasn't an empty home, it was a fresh start, a chance to be renewed, an opportunity to rebuild according to God's plan and not for survival, security, or stability. I'd be building for God's purpose and I'd be okay because I had God.

Ephesians 4:23 "Be constantly renewed in the mind..."

Seated Indian style in the middle of my empty living room clutching my journal with the words, **Dream Big**, emblazoned on the cover, I began to flip the pages searching for where I'd written lists of scriptures that helped me when I felt afraid. Scanning the list with my index finger, I found it:

Hebrews 13:6 "So we say with confidence,
The Lord is my helper so I will have no fear."

Although I'd be facing a few thunderstorms and wasn't clear about what to do next, I remembered that God had always been with me and he blessed me with a powerful tool – my mouth. So, whatever was ahead, as long as I had God and my mouth, I'd be okay. It's funny how God has to strip us down to the bare bones in order to get our attention, but sitting with my journal in my lap in my empty space, God had my full attention.

Journaling is my form of therapy. It gives me an outlet to express my thoughts and feelings so that I can understand what I'm going through more clearly. It proves to be an extension of prayer and helps me focus on scripture. During my soul searching, journaling helped me see that my entire situation wasn't about Evan or Aunt Elsie. I'd never be able to change them; that was God's job. My job, however, was to change me. Using prayer to converse with God and journaling to flesh out those conversations, I'm able to find clarity. Each day I read scriptures and speak them aloud. Spending time with God through prayer and journaling is my lifeline.

My latest journal session gave me strength, so after I'd written the last word and closed the book, I rose from the floor and paced my new residence speaking **Hebrews 13:6** to erase my fears. Blessing every square inch of my unfurnished space, I repeated it until all fear vanished. My words held power and could speak life over my circumstances instead of allowing my circumstances to speak life over me. Exhaustion kicked in from all my pacing and I dropped to my knees, in the middle of the living room, to declare my trust in God wholeheartedly. Every move I made from that point on would be intentional. I could get a handle on my mouth and once again use it for my good. My words would no longer be a result of my gut reaction, defense, or survival. My steering wheel was handed over to God and he was about to take full control.

CHAPTER 16

Earlier that day, I'd unintentionally come across **Mark 11:25**. As a matter of fact, I tried to skim past it because I was searching for something else, but my hand slowed down and my eyes went straight to this verse. That happened often when prayer journaling. I'd think I was looking for one thing and God would take me to another section. So, I knew God was pointing me to that word for a reason. Eventually, I found out why.

Forgiveness

Still fighting a private battle with vengeance and retribution, I needed another journal therapy session. I knew that vengeance wasn't mine, it was God's. I couldn't allow the desire for revenge to control me. For so long, I was stuck in a place of confusion on when to speak and when to shut up. Was my mouth too silent during the years I spent with Aunt Elsie or was it too aggressive during the years I spent with Evan? Journaling gave me a judgment-free zone to sort through my flaws and analyze my mistakes. Admittedly, I'd chosen both Aunt Elsie and Evan out of my desire to find stability and security, much like my father did when he chose my mother. History has a strange way of repeating itself especially through generational curses. Like Daddy, this choice cost me plenty of pain, heartache, and wasted years.

Lingering anger still held space in my soul and I knew I had to do something about it, so I prayed. Sorting my prayer out through journaling, I discovered that I needed to take a long hard look at my heart. Had it been hardened? Who was I holding things against? Shoot! The more I thought about it, I had a laundry list of people.

For two weeks straight, each time I sat down to prayer journal, my Bible, opened to **Mark 11:25**. God was trying to tell me something. I needed to forgive. Forgive everyone who I was holding something in my heart against. I realized that forgiveness isn't fair. It's not based on whether or not a person deserves it. An inability to forgive is the one tried and true barrier to joy. Even though I didn't want to admit it. Mama was first on the list.

Mark 11:25 - "And when you stand praying, if you hold anything against anyone forgive them..."

Forgiving Mama

Though I was now an adult, she and I had no relationship. Bitterness had caused her to shut herself off from the world. During our court battles, she was ready to fight for her man to the bitter end, but Daddy's plea bargain felt like betrayal. Even though she knew he was innocent, his plea deal hurt her pride and made her look like a fool.

Too proud to admit that she'd made mistakes, she preferred to withdraw from everyone including me. Mama was angry with the world and believed we caused her failed relationships. Over the years, I witnessed how Mama's anger formed a cancer on her heart and impaired her relationship with me. The inability to forgive puts a block in your relationship with God and I wanted everything God promised me. Time to make amends.

Calling Mama was one of the hardest phone calls I'd ever made. However, I had to find a way to forgive her. Holding my breath with each ring, I anxiously waited for her to answer. Finally, she did.

"Hello." Her voice still sounded like she ingested stale cigarette smoke every day.

"Hey Mama, it's Kira."

Seconds passed before she said, "Hey baby."

Tears poured down my face and couldn't get any words. I could hear Mama crying as well. After talking and crying for hours, there was one question that kept eating at me.

"Mama, why did you refuse to divorce Daddy to get me back?"

Pausing long enough to gather her words, she said, "I really don't know how to explain it other than to paint you a picture. Imagine if our family was in a boat in the middle of the ocean filled with sharks and I'm the only one who can swim. Your dad falls off the boat, so I have to jump in and save him."

Silently, I questioned her logic. So you jump over and leave your kids on a boat all alone in the middle of the ocean? What if one of the kids falls in? What if you die trying to save him and we're left without a mother or a father? Who was going to be there for us? Who would protect us from the sharks and the unknown?

I didn't voice my inner thoughts because forgiveness isn't about the other person. Forgiveness is about freeing yourself to receive the blessings that God has for you. As long as there's a grudge, there's a wedge between you and God. I was on a mission to forgive so that I could escape the anger in my heart. I forgave her that day for not fighting for me.

Forgiving Daddy

Long before our family crisis, God had been trying to get my father's attention. Daddy had been my hero, and being so young, I didn't know the signs of a drug user. Long before I was taken from home, Daddy's life had already begun to spin out of control. Drugs had taken over. His addiction was one of the reasons he couldn't keep a steady job and was always hounding Mama for money. Wrongful imprisonment, on a trumped up lie, was God's way of getting his attention.

Immediately after serving his six-month sentence, Daddy turned to the streets to cope with his pain and the stress that our family tragedy caused him. For the first few years of me being in foster care, I held on to the excuse that Daddy was a victim and that's why he couldn't help me. When I turned fourteen, I discovered he was a drug addict living on the streets and peddling for money.

While riding to South DeKalb Mall with my friends one weekend, I spotted him. His was the face out of a million faces. It was Daddy. He'd aged tremendously and walked with a cane but I recognized him. He was peddling for money off the Interstate exit ramp near Flat Shoals Road. Eager to see him and talk, I asked my friend to pull over at the curb. Recognizing his baby girl immediately, his whole face lit up. Standing in disbelief, I watched him try to pretend like nothing had happened as he greeted me by my nickname. The moniker brought back such pleasant memories – momentarily.

"Cutie Pie, what are you doing out here? Look how you've grown."

He was trying to protect me the best way he could think of by pretending everything was all right but my heart was broken the moment I saw him. Why didn't he come for me? He didn't deserve to lose his family, freedom, and then end up homeless, but why didn't he come save me once he was released? Sadness silenced me. Now that I knew he had a choice and didn't choose me, I couldn't forgive him.

My unwillingness to forgive Daddy had morphed into anger, shame, and unworthiness. Deep down, I wrestled with trying to understand how drugs could be more important than me. When I had come upon this journey to forgive, I remembered I didn't know how to get into touch with him. The last time I had seen him, he lived on the streets. Through prayer journaling, my mind and heart were open to forgiveness. Once we are open to something, it flows right to us. One day, out of the clear blue sky, God gave me my chance.

While in the grocery store, Daddy was heavy on my mind. So much so, I heard a voice a couple of aisles over that sounded just like him. Thinking my mind was playing tricks on me, I tried to ignore it. Pushing my grocery cart down the aisle searching for Ragu sauce, I paused midstride. Right before me was Daddy in one of those motorized wheelchairs they usually have in the front of the grocery store. He called me by my nickname and gave me a familiar wide smile. I remembered that grin from my childhood. Approaching him, I could see that he'd aged quite a bit, but he looked better than I'd ever seen him and he smelled like Brut cologne. He was no longer a gaunt shell of the Daddy I used to know. He'd gained weight, was clean shaven, and looked like half a million bucks. Dead smack in the middle of the aisle, we chatted for hours catching up with one another. Clean, off drugs, and back on his feet, he admitted how he'd been trying to get in touch with me. He wanted to re-establish a relationship.

Guard still up, I was hesitant at first. Still, we exchanged telephone numbers and stayed in contact. During our regular talks, Daddy shared with me how God had given him grace and mercy. Our conversations were light hearted and Daddy was still his humorous self. However, there was one time that his jokes and playfulness subsided. Daddy was very serious.

"Kira, I want you to forgive me," he said. "I apologize for abandoning you, leaving you without my protection, guidance, and love. I can't imagine what you went through and I don't think I'm strong enough to handle your truth. My heart ached for you every day even out on the streets when I thought that you were out there growing up without me." Tears once again streamed down my face and the only response I could muster in that moment came effortlessly. "Daddy, you're forgiven."

Forgiving my father enabled me to focus on enjoying the now instead of lingering on the past and what I might have missed. As long as he now shows concern for me and my family, shares his wisdom, talks to me about God, and we share plenty of laughter, then nothing else matters anymore. What if I hadn't decided to forgive him for being irresponsible and for being absent from my life? I would have blocked the blessing of having this wonderful relationship with him now. Through my prayer journal, I understood how forgiveness allows God to handle our situations. God will always restore things to their proper order. It took nearly thirty years for me to become the daughter that God intended for me to be but God's plan will always prevail. Nothing put together by the Lord can be torn apart. I still don't know why I was taken away from my family at ten-years-old other than it was God's will so that I could be who I am today. God has a purpose for my life and he has one for your life too.

Great things were underway. Amazing releases and amazing shifts were happening each day. Flipping back to the page in my journal that contained my forgiveness list, next up was Andrea.

Forgiving Andrea

Sister – your first best friend. Big sister – your first mentor. Andrea was neither. Although in touch with one another, we were practically strangers. Subconsciously, I'd limited her access to my life. Deep, in the part of my heart that I sometimes wished wasn't there, was a grudge. I hated Andrea. Her lie had ruined my life and changed its entire course. Her selfishness had sacrificed the two most important relationships that a child has with anyone on Earth. Because of her, I'd lost my mother and father. How could I not hold a grudge?

Was our sisterhood, or the lack thereof, one of my stumbling blocks? After years of wondering, I'd decided to get too the root of the issue. With two long breaths, I dialed Andrea's cell phone. I needed closure. I asked God to be a guard over my mouth and help me choose the right words.

"Hi Sis," Andrea said after picking up on the third ring.

"Hey." Silence after my greeting as I decided what to say next. Our last conversation ended in screaming, and neither of us had the energy for another round of that. Since I'd made the phone call, it was on me to speak.

"Andrea, I wish we were closer and could talk to one another, like sisters. Trust each other."

"You can trust me," she responded, somewhat offended. "I've always been there for you. Protecting you the best way I could. But you say some really mean things sometimes."

"I know. I'm sorry. For years, I've been angry with you for everything that happened to us growing up. I know it wasn't all your fault but I did blame you."

"Yeah, I know you did. I was young and angry with Mama for choosing Daniel over me. All I wanted was for her to love me and put me first. Instead, she just threw all her responsibilities on me. I was the one who wiped your butt and combed your hair, remember?" Her voice softened. "I loved you. You were my baby sister. I didn't mean for you to get caught up in my mess. Didn't mean for Daniel to go through all that. I just wanted out."

Hearing her say those words was all I needed. The door to forgiveness was open when I dialed her number and her apology helped me walk through it. All my feelings had been laid out in my journal. My writing had primed me for forgiveness and readied my heart to move past that stumbling block.

We chatted a little longer and shared some sisterly laughter. Our relationship had taken a stab but forgiveness was the medicine. Now the question was, whether there was any medicine strong enough to help me forgive Grandma Helen.

Forgiving Grandma Helen

For days, I tried to journal about her. About the pain she'd caused me. However, I'd be staring at a blank page. I felt nothing. How could I forgive someone who'd been a real life Boogie Man? I didn't know which feelings were stronger so I just wrote down a list of them all:

Fear.

Pain.

Hate.

Revenge.

Memories of those hard, hate-filled eyes lingered around my head. As a little girl, she invoked so much fear, I'd almost pee my pants. She'd taken advantage of my childlike vulnerability. My weakness. My inability to fight back. Forgiveness was nowhere in my heart. Just as I started to get second thoughts on forgiving the vilest person I've ever known, my cell phone rang. Guess whose name scrolled across the screen? Grandma Helen. Why was she calling me? She never called me. In fact, we barely spoke. Somehow or another, her number was scrolling across my phone. It was God. I'd be facing this sooner than I planned.

Hesitantly, I picked up the phone. "Hello?"

"Kira, this is Grandma Helen, baby." She spoke in a sweet voice that she only used when she wanted something.

Way past the pleasantries, I wanted to get straight to the point. "Hi, Grandma Helen. What brings you to call?"

"Grandma needs a favor. Can you open a bank account for me in your name? Uncle Sam will take the little money I've saved up for my retirement if I don't move it into another account."

"Why didn't you ask Andrea?"

"She already has one in her name."

"No," I responded. "I'm not going to do that."

Stunned and no longer in her conniving sweet voice she said, "Why?!"

"Well, since you ask…" I was ready to let her finally feel the wrath of my mouth. "You must think I forgot all you did to me as a little girl. You hate me. You hated my Daddy too. You were the puppet master behind Andrea's lies. You didn't think I knew that, did you? You destroyed our family. You scheme and you destroy. And now you have the nerve to ask me to do something for you?"

The more I spoke, the more she morphed back into the real Grandma Helen.

"You lil 'yella heifer. You think you getting me told, don't you? I can still slap the taste out of your mouth!"

"See," I interrupted, "there you go thinking everything's about you. I'm not getting you told. I'm telling you the truth. And now I know for sure, you're really as crazy as I thought. I was planning to call you so that I could find a way to forgive you, but you know what? I don't need to forgive you because I don't feel anything toward you other than pity. God is going to take care of you. There'll be a warm seat in hell with your name on it and that's a good enough reason for me to forgive you. And, don't call my phone number again. Goodbye!"

As I ended the call, a weight lifted off me. Everything that had been pent inside was now free. I realized Grandma

Helen's page in my journal stayed blank because I didn't feel anything. There was nothing to resolve or forgive. My conscience was clear. God would take care of her.

Forgiving Evan

Evan was simply the wrong man. He was simply a mistake that needed correcting. I didn't verbally forgive him, I simply let go of the animosity I harvested in my heart for him. Releasing my regrets for marrying Evan was the gateway to my blessings and opened my heart to love. Little did I know, it was also the final step toward finding my happily ever after.

CHAPTER 17

My decision to marry Evan made me second guess my ability to choose the right man. As I journaled, I questioned if I'd know when I found the right one once he finally came along. If so, would I be able to keep my mouth shut long enough to keep him? But, what I learned was when you find the one, YOU WILL KNOW because he'll bring you closer to God. Now, if only I could shut my mouth, the story would end here, but since I can't, here's the long answer.

Exiting the stadium of a high school football game, I heard a voice say, "Excuse me, may I talk to you for a minute?"

Feeling a bit annoyed from getting approached by so many guys that night, I turned around with an attitude. "What?!"

Unmoved by my aggressive stance, the polite voice spoke up again. "Do you have a minute? Are you in a hurry?"

Finally, I turned around and froze at the sight before me. At a loss of words, I couldn't get anything to come out of my mouth, which is a huge feat because normally I'd always have something to say.

He then extended his hand and said, "Hi, I'm Mark. I know you're in a hurry, but do you have a business card or anything so that I can get in touch with you?"

His asking about my business card snapped me out of my trance. I'd almost left home without them but a voice reminded me to run back in and get them in case I had a sales lead. Now, what were the chances that he'd ask for a business card? Not my phone number but a business card! Thank God I had gone back and got them before I left the house. As fate would have it, he happened to be the same guy I had a huge crush on in high school. He was a senior when I was a freshman, so he didn't even remember me but I sure hadn't forgotten him.

Handing him my card, I said, "I know you. You used to hang out with Clark, Donald, and a bunch of other dudes. You had a Starter suit for everyday of the week and always had a notebook in your hand as you leaned against the lockers."

Now, most guys would've thought I was some sort of stalker to have remembered all of those details. I'm sure some may have even been spooked and ran for the hills. But hey, I said I had a crush on him so of course I remembered. However, it didn't seem to faze him one bit. Instead, he stood there and smiled back at me. I was used to guys staring at me but his gaze made my heart flutter. There was no lust in his eyes. He looked as if he was trying to read my soul.

It seemed in that moment, during what might have only been a two-minute exchange, like time was standing still and that we were the only people in attendance. As if, no one else was around and that we weren't in the middle of a crowded football game. I heard nothing and saw no one else but him. Our souls were communicating a language that only we could understand. As we held each other's gaze, I knew there was something different and very special about this man. Finally drums from the marching band broke me out of my hypnotized stupor and we parted ways. Was that love at first sight?

Unfortunately, my old insecurities of not being good enough were trying to creep in. Immediately, I was afraid of what I'd just experienced. Is he ***The One***?

How To Know If He Is The One

He won't play mind games. Mark called me that night just like he said he would. He wanted to make sure that I made it to my car safely so he checked on me within minutes of walking away. His tone was sincere concern, something to which I had never grown accustomed. No one had cared about my safety since I was ten-years-old. This blew me away.

That night, I prayed and journaled about the whole experience. Expressing my feelings so openly made me realize I'd never prayed about a relationship before it became a relationship. By the time I prayed about my marriage to Evan, our union was already doomed.

As I journaled, I knew the next man I married would bring me closer to God even though I didn't fully understand exactly what that meant. That's the thing about journaling. It will have you exploring areas of your mind and heart that previously weren't topics you'd ordinarily think about. I already had a strong prayer life plus my journaling increased the effectiveness of it so how could this guy, or any guy for that matter, bring me closer? My brain was moving quickly. I mean, I had just met him and was already evaluating him as a husband. I didn't really intend to pursue a new relationship. Since I was still putting my own pieces together, I couldn't understand why those thoughts were in my mind but because I had a relationship with God, he was preparing me for my future.

Mark and I began to date and he always kept his word. If he asked me out, he showed up for every date. Yet, a part of me was always expecting him to let me down.

He'll rise to the standard you set. Now fiercely independent, I'd adopted a no-tolerance-for-foolishness policy. A woman on a mission who was determined to never stop being me or hold my tongue to get, have, or keep a man. Headed out for our standing Thursday date night, there was tension in the air when I got in Mark's car. He was visibly agitated and frustrated. We stopped for gas and he handed me a twenty-dollar bill gesturing for me to go in and pay for the gas. Thinking that was quite rude, I said "No, you're taking me on a date, so I shouldn't be going in and paying for gas."

The most important thing about wisdom is learning from past mistakes and in previous relationships I hadn't established how I expected to be treated. I just went along with whatever. Irritated with my response, Mark jumped out the car and paid for the gas but returned still visibly irritated. Maybe he'd had a bad day yet that didn't matter to me. I expected to be treated a certain way – bad day or not.

As we approached the side of the gas station to exit, I looked over at him and said in a curt tone, "You can make a left and take me home."

Surely, I hadn't come out to deal with a bad mood and reasoned I could have had a better time sitting on my bed, enjoying my own company with a nice bowl of Fruity Pebbles cereal. Needless to say, he made a right turn, and we continued on our date. We enjoyed the rest of the evening and shared laughs about the whole incident. He'd had a bad day and was frustrated about an issue with an important client but, amid his 'tude, I had set a standard of how I expected to be treated and Mark rose to it. Finally, I loved myself enough to be willing to go back home and enjoy my own company instead of tolerating mistreatment.

His actions will speak louder than any words. After taking my sons to the mall to purchase new sneakers, I headed to the parking lot with both boys in tow. We were laughing and chatting until my SUV wouldn't start after several turns of the ignition. Darkness was approaching fast so I immediately called AAA. Then, my phone rang and it was Mark on the other end. I told him all about my car ordeal and how I was stuck at the empty mall with my sons. It took moving Heaven and Earth to convince him not to come to the rescue because AAA would be arriving at any moment. Finally, Mark agreed to stay back but first he quizzed me about the car as he diagnosed the problem over the phone. He said it seemed like I needed a battery and possibly an alternator. He wasn't a mechanic so I took his diagnosis as just a man being a man and wanting to save a damsel in distress but would leave the real outcome to the automobile professionals.

Somehow, though, Mark must have read my thoughts as he then said, "Don't worry about the alternator. I'll take care of that. And I'm headed to get a battery for you now."

Sitting in the front seat of the tow truck as it approached my home, I could see Mark's car parked outside my gate. He was already waiting. Whipping his car in, right behind the AAA truck, he quickly jumped out and took over the entire situation. I stood on the sidewalk watching him handle the things as if it was his car that wouldn't crank. After engaging car talk with the tow driver, Mark's prediction proved to be accurate – it was my battery. I was worried because it was the thick of night and there wasn't enough light in the parking lot for him to put it in. That didn't stop Mark though. He changed the battery using only the flashlight from his cell phone. He then asked me to get in and crank it. The engine turned over immediately.

I bubbled with gratitude. "Thank you so much. No one has ever gone out of their way like this to help me."

Once he stopped tinkering under the hood, he gave me the same intense stare as the night he met me. "You don't have to thank me," he replied. "God willing, you'll never have a problem that I can't handle."

Every hair on my neck stood up with shivers. His words sent chills down my spine. Mark didn't ask to come inside the house that night. He just held me for a while, right there in the dark parking lot, outside in the cold. Deep down, I knew he was The One but I still didn't want to believe it.

He'll take everything to God. Mark and I had our first real misunderstanding within a few months of dating. Being a successful businessman, a handsome one at that, I knew he had plenty of clients, some of them female. One night, over dinner, his phone rang several times. Curios, I glanced at his phone each time it rang. The name Misty scrolled across the screen and Mark excused himself from the table. After what seemed like forever he abruptly ended our date.

"I have a family emergency," he claimed.

All my sensors went to high alert. Did he really have a family emergency and who is Misty? Old habits die hard and subconsciously I'd wondered if I was good enough for Mark. He was a successful entrepreneur and I was a divorcee with two children living in a scantily furnished home.

Going along with what I presumed was game, I simply replied, "Ok. We haven't ordered yet, so let's just pay for the drinks and go."

The ride back was unusually quiet. Good conversation and laughter had become our cornerstone, but after receiving that phone call from Misty, Mark's whole demeanor changed. We said our goodbyes and he promised to call me the next day. Mentally, I was done. I didn't have time for games. I just knew he was too good to be true.

Refusing to answer his call for weeks, I used that incident as a reason to shut down and push him away. Then one day I heard what something tapping my bedroom window. Initially, I thought it was just the wind so I ignored it. However, the sound continued and each tap sounded louder than the former.

Bothered, I peeped out the window to see what it was. That's when I saw him, in all his splendor. Mark was two stories down and throwing pebbles. A smile spread across my face but I was too stubborn to open the window. Clearly persistence was one of his strong points because he kept tossing pebbles. Finally, I opened it.

Staring up at me as though I was Rapunzel trapped in a castle, he said, "Well you left me no choice, you wouldn't answer the phone. Please come down and give me five minutes."

Deep down, I was flattered to have a man go through such drastic measures to talk to me. I mean, my own Daddy had never thrown pebbles at the foster home windows. This was a first for me.

I slipped on my shoes and went downstairs to hear him out. With a subtle hint of arrogance, I declared, "Your five minutes starts now."

Expecting him to go into a Keith Sweat, *please baby, baby please* speech, he surprised me by doing the opposite. He grabbed my hands while asking me to bow my head, and said "Let's pray."

That sealed the deal for me and the only bigger confirmation would've been Jesus coming down from Heaven and telling me himself. Mark asked God to show him how to be the man that God wanted him to be. He also asked God to heal us of any past issues that might hinder our relationship. He prayed about being a good husband to me, which by the way, made me crack an eye open because I couldn't believe he was thinking that way. He asked God to bless him to have me as his wife one day.

I saw him in a way I had seen no other man. He was a man of God. He was a man who prayed and was not ashamed to be vulnerable in front of me as he bared his soul. He was a man who wasn't afraid to do what was necessary to have the woman he felt God had sent him. Mark inspired me to have an even better relationship with God which then propelled me to want to be a wife. Not just any type of wife, I wanted to be a Godly wife. Honestly, he had my attention at ***let's pray*** but he had my whole heart by the time he said Amen.

As it turns out, Misty was his sister and their mother had been rushed to the hospital.

He'll help you grow as a person. Mark brings out the best in me. He helps me uncover talents and gifts I had previously been too insecure to share with others. Astonished by all my journals, he asked if I could write grants and proposals. He had new clients and needed assistance. Mark believed in my writing abilities even before I did. Petrified that I'd blow one of his deals, I tried to refuse. However, his confidence in me never wavered. With no formal training and only by God's ***grace***, my writing talents flourished and were the missing component Mark needed for his business to sky rocket. Proposal after proposal was well received and we were awarded grants for his nonprofit organization. Mark brought out talents and skills that had been dormant and untapped. Not only was he helping me grow spiritually but also professionally.

He'll be strong enough to lead you. Mark is led by God. I know this for a fact because I see him spend time in prayer. This insight keeps me from mouthing off, even when I don't agree with his decisions. Don't get me wrong, this is a daily challenge. Instead of verbalizing my disagreement or carrying an attitude in my body language, I pray about those concerns and ask God to show Mark the right way. Then, I vent my frustrations through journaling. When I shut my mouth, I'm showing respect to my husband and to God's perfect design for marriage because the husband is the head of the wife.

CHAPTER 18

Finally.... Kira

Everything that happens to us as children makes us who we are as adults, good or bad. My perfectly imperfect life is a living testimony. Believing God at his word and having a joyful spirit has enabled me to overcome every situation. God's glory is always shining on me. That's what others see. Sometimes they hate me because of it but it doesn't bother me as much anymore. God has given me wisdom and peace to allow him to fight my battles. I am also wise enough now to limit my interactions with negative, jealous, and hateful people. By refusing to allow my joy to be hindered because of someone else's unhappiness, I've taken control. Others can stew in their misery by themselves. But for me? I'm going to keep smiling in spite of it all.

I don't worry about things like I had in the past. My relationship with God has strengthened so much that fear has no place in my life. I give it to God. Anything that makes me afraid, I face it head on because I know God is with me. I pray about it and then I fight that fear with faith. I know it's God's will for us to be in peace and anything that makes us afraid blocks our peace. I was afraid to go against the District Attorney, my caseworker, and every other adult I had encountered, but even as a little girl, I had faith the size of a mustard seed. So, if I can have faith at such a young age, surely I can have it at forty something.

I was afraid to leave a lifeless, faithless, and Godless marriage. So, I prayed about it and God saw me through. I was afraid when other people tried to tell me that I would have a hard time raising boys as a single mom but I had faith and God gave me strength and wisdom to raise them. Then, as a bonus, he sent them a father-figure. Fearing divorce, I was afraid to marry again until God sent Mark. I have trusted God and had faith through adversity, challenges, and trials. Each time I found peace.

Living joyfully is not self-medicating because that only covers the symptoms. Living joyfully is self-healing which is a long-term cure. My joy and my peace are non-negotiable and if anything comes along to jeopardize either, it has to go. I'm perfectly content with people not liking my resolve. When I feel static cropping up on my joy station, I change the channel or at the bare minimum turn the volume down to limit my exposure. So long to negativity. Bye-Bye to my haters. The only person responsible for my joy is me. God gives it to us freely, we just have to make the decision to value it enough to protect it. Don't accept your life in the condition that it is in when you know you need to make a change. Get up, switch gears, interrupt the chaos, and go get your joy.

When I reflect over the last forty plus years of my life, I'm still amazed by God's ***grace.*** I know for sure that God intends for us to use our lives as a ministry to others. The best way for me to do this is by speaking my truth and sharing the wisdom I've learned along the way. That's my purpose. Many years ago, I made a promise to myself that when I could have a say-so over my life, I would never allow anyone to silence me. It took God to show me how to use my voice and it takes prayer for me to continue to use my mouth in the way that he intended. As I have grown wiser, I have learned that I can speak volumes by not saying anything and instead look to God to speak up for me or at least show me his perfect timing.

Now believe me, I still have lapses where I don't always do this. Sometimes, the timing isn't right. Even if you're being honest, some people aren't ready or mature enough for the truth. Therefore, I'm still learning discernment when it comes to shutting my big mouth.

Job 8:21 - "He will once again fill your mouth with laughter and your lips with shouts of joy..."